Where can you find these pieces of the past in San Francisco?

To Kathyrn Otoshi,
with deep appreciation
for all your help and support.

Text and illustrations copyright © 2016 Marissa Moss
Cover and internal design by Simon Stahl
Original series design by Liz Demeter/Demeter Design ©2012 Sourcebooks, Inc.
Original series cover design concept by Brittany Vibbert, Sourcebooks

Published by Creston Books, LLC in Berkeley, California
www.crestonbooks.co

CIP data for this book is available from the Library of Congress.

Source of Production: Worzalla Books, Stevens Point, Wisconsin
Printed and bound in the United States of America
1 2 3 4 5

CALIFORNIA
DREAMING
Mira's Diary

CALIFORNIA DREAMING
Mira's Diary

By Marissa Moss

Creston Books

July 10

Usually I start a brand new journal with a brand new post-card, a picture of where I'll travel to next. But this time I'm starting with a drawing of what's right in front of me. Because it's pretty spectacular.

Much better than looking right next to me, at my oh-so-furious brother. We're finally doing something fun, taking a ride on the giant Ferris wheel in London, and he looks ready to kill me.

"Come on, Malcolm, enjoy yourself! Be a normal tourist!"

"I wish! You're ruining everything!"

"What did I do?" As if it's my fault that we're chasing Mom all over the place. My fault that I can time-travel and he can't. I didn't choose this!

"It's what you didn't do and you know it!"

I stare out of the glass pod, blinking back tears. People are tiny blobs of color, cars moving paint splashes. London is small from so high up, like a collage. I try to imagine what it would have looked like a century ago. That should be easy, since I was just there, but I can't picture it from this height. From this time.

"If it were up to me," Malcolm continues, "we'd be home by now. This would all be over."

I don't need to be reminded that I've failed so far. That I haven't convinced Mom to come back. When I'd first time-traveled, I was told the rules. There aren't many, but they're super important:

You can't bring back anything from the past.

You can't let people in the past know your real identity.

You can't change the past – you can only observe.

Family members shouldn't travel together because that increases the risk they'll change something in their own future. That's why Mom sends me messages, but refuses to ever meet me.

So how can I argue with her if she runs away whenever she sees me?

The glass pod lurches lower, bringing the spires closer.

"Are you crying?" Malcolm peers at me. "Don't be a crybaby!"

"Don't be a bully!" I snap. That shuts him up. Normally Malcolm is a sweet, protective older brother. He's helped me a lot, even if he's stuck in the present while I travel into the past, looking for Mom. But he's fed up with me now. Mom's mad at me and so is Malcolm. Dad is just disappointed.

My stomach dips as the wheel turns again. The ground moves closer and the dots of color grow arms and legs, turn into people.

At first, I'd believed Mom that past injustices needed correcting and I'd helped her. We were fixing things, terrible wrongs that should be righted. I felt like a super-hero, popping in and out of centuries. Postcards from Mom had pointed us where to go, from Paris to Rome to London.

This last time, I met Arthur Conan Doyle, the famous writer who created Sherlock Holmes. And that changed everything. He was a time-traveler too, and he explained our responsibilities better than anyone. He thought Mom was trying to protect my future by altering the past. And that's wrong. More than wrong, it's dangerous.

The problem is, Mom's too busy trying to protect me to listen to me.

The glass pod glides down to the ground. Malcolm doesn't even look at me as he clambers out. So much for normal tourist fun.

Dad is waiting for us by the edge of the river. He doesn't look any happier than my brother, but he gives a fake smile.

"What next?" he chirps. "Want to see the changing of the guard?"

Malcolm rolls his eyes.

"You have a better idea?" Dad drops the false cheeriness, which is a huge improvement.

"We're just filling time until Mom sends another postcard," Malcolm complains. "Why don't we go home?"

"You don't think I can bring her back, do you?" I feel my face heat up with shame and anger.

"No, actually, I don't."

"Stop fighting, you two!" Dad barks. "We have to stick together as a family! That's the only way to get Mom home. I know it's frustrating that we mostly watch and wait while Mira takes all the risks, but that's just the way it is."

"Takes all the risks? How about has all the fun! And what do I get? A stupid baby ride on a Ferris wheel!"

Dad puts an arm around Malcolm, even though he has to reach up to do it since Malcolm's latest growth spurt. "We're the research team, okay? Maybe not as glamorous as your sister's job, but important just the same."

"Anyway, you're right." I smile at my brother, trying to soften him up. "We need to go home. To Berkeley." Mom said she has one last, best chance to change the Horrible Thing that will happen in our future. That has to happen closer, both in time and in place, to our lives today. It makes sense, right?"

We're walking along the edge of the river, heading toward Big Ben. Keeping my eye on the tall clock tower, I feel as if Time itself is guiding me.

"I'm not convinced Mom is in Berkeley, though that would be convenient," Dad says. "What ever happened there that mattered enough to change? Nothing."

"What about the whole Free Speech Movement?" Malcolm objects. "And the anti-war protests of the '60s and '70s? And wasn't there that famous kidnapping of Patty Hearst, the newspaper heiress, by the Symbionese Liberation army?"

"Wow!" Dad's impressed. "You know your Berkeley history."

"I go to Berkeley High, Dad." Malcolm snorts. "Where Indigenous Peoples Day and International Women's Day are holidays. Students celebrate women's achievements by making mothers take a day off work to stay home and take care of them."

"Mom's not dealing with any of that stuff," I say. "And she's not in Berkeley. She'll be in San Francisco. And I don't know what time she's going to, just where. Once I find a Touchstone to take me into the past, I'll figure it out."

"And here I thought you'd be dressed like a hippy and talking Power to the People. Wait a minute." Malcolm grins. "You could be selling those T-shirts on Telegraph Avenue, the Yes-to-Anarchy ones. Maybe you'll be on Alcatraz when the Native Americans tried to occupy it, take it back as their land."

"I don't think that's it," I mumble, horrified at the thought of wearing tie-dyed anything.

"Why not?" Malcolm presses. "Every time you've gone back, Mom's wanted some horrible injustice righted. The way the governor tear-gassed anti-war protestors was terrible. And what could be more unfair than how Native Americans were treated? If I could go back in time, I'd join both those protests." His voice takes on an angry edge again. For the zillionth time, I wish he'd been the one to inherit the time-traveling gene. He's the one who's so passionate about history. I know he's thinking the same thing.

"Won't time-travel be tricky back home?" Dad asks. "Touch-stones are old, historical stuff. What's old in San Francisco? Not much." Dad leans on the railing, looking across to Tower Bridge, a much older bridge than any in California.

"How do we know Touchstones have to be ancient? Can't there be brand spanking-new ones?"

"I've been wondering about the whole Touchstone thing. Who creates them and how?" Malcolm asks. "Maybe that's my secret power – I can create Touchstones! You should ask Mom's time-traveling friend next time, that Walrus-mustache fellow."

"You mean Morton? He's not particularly generous with information." Really, he's not generous with anything. He does the bare minimum as a favor to Mom. And I don't want to disappoint Malcolm with yet another mystery talent he doesn't have.

"If you find Morton, ask him about Mom, not the Touchstones," Dad orders. "We have to stay focused on what matters here. Once Mom's home, you can ask her about the Touchstones."

Dad takes off his glasses and cleans them with his shirt, a nervous tic he has. He's more than worried. He's afraid. Now that he's seen the Watcher here in London, he's more freaked out than ever. She's not an abstract enemy stuck in the past, but a living person who came to our present, threatening Malcolm and me. Dad's seen how strong the Watcher is. And how determined. And maybe that's why he gives in – to get us away from her.

I just hope she won't follow us home.

July 14

As soon as we step out of the airport at SFO, even though there's nothing to see but taxis, shuttles, cars, and asphalt, the air smells crisper, cleaner. I swallow big gulps, tasting the fresh Pacific breezes. For a second, I forget the tough job ahead. I just want to go home, have some Zachary's pizza, and see my friends. I'd love to forget all this time-travel stuff and be a normal kid again. Well, as normal as I can be.

Malcolm stretches out his arms, as if he's welcoming the California-ness. "Just feel that delicious fog! So we haven't missed a do-nothing summer after all. Now's our chance!"

Dad stuffs our bags into the taxi at the head of the line. "How can you think about relaxing? Have you forgotten about your mother?"

"How could I? You and Mira won't let me! You've both

hijacked my summer. The traveling part was okay. I like seeing new countries, but now we're back home, which means the excitement is over."

"Maybe for you!" I snap.

"Stop it, you two, and get into the cab," Dad orders. We're just one big grouchy family, returning from vacation.

We haven't been gone that long, weeks only, but it feels much longer and I'm excited to see that our house looks exactly the same. It's dusty and stuffy from being shut up, but still familiar and comfortable. Dad goes out for groceries while Malcolm and I sit down to brainstorm. When we were little, we used to pore over those big picture books, searching for the red-striped figure, hunting for Waldo. Now we don't have a book, but we still need to find someone. The question is where, or rather, when is Mom?

 "You keep insisting that Mom's in San Francisco, but I still think Berkeley is possible. Tell me why it's not." Malcolm turns on his computer and starts searching, not even waiting for any suggestions from me.

"So you're going to help me?" I hate arguing with Malcolm. Mostly because I never win.

"Do I have a choice?"

"Of course you do! You could ignore me entirely."

"Like Dad would let me." He keeps his eyes on the screen, blocking me out.

"Please, Malcolm, don't make me beg! You're doing this for Mom, not me."

"I'm doing it for both of you! For all of us!" And now he does look at me. "So let's figure it out."

"Okay, here's what I think. We know that the Terrible Thing involves us, so it has to happen here, where we live. And the place with the most history nearby is San Francisco."

"So that's why you think San Francisco, just because it has more history than Berkeley?"

"Humor me, okay?"

Malcolm starts searching, though he doesn't know what to look for any more than I do. "Stop breathing over my shoulder!" he says, more annoyed than ever. "Give me a chance to see what major events happened."

"The 1906 earthquake?" I pull up a chair next to his, determined to be nice. "There's not much Mom could change with that. How do you stop a quake from happening?"

Malcolm scrolls quickly down a page. "Not the earthquake itself, but afterwards. The main damage wasn't caused by the quake. It was the fires afterwards that flattened the city."

"But Mom can't change that, either. Weren't the fires hard to put out because water mains all over the city broke? There wasn't any water to put them out, except what they pumped from the bay using fire boats."

"That was part of the problem. But what made the fires way worse than they would have been was completely controlled by people. That could be Mom's event. Maybe she's trying to keep San Francisco from burning down."

"How would she do that?"

"Stop the dynamiting. Or make sure they did it right, not stupidly, the way they actually did. The army didn't have explosives experts in the city, so they didn't know what they were doing. Instead of creating fire breaks with the dynamite, they ended up sparking more fires. Half the city was lost because of the army."

It sounds like the kind of impossible quest Mom would love. She'd have to either steal all the dynamite, sabotage it, or convince military officials they don't know what they're doing. I can't imagine a general listening to a woman, not now and definitely not in 1906.

"Wait a minute," I grumble. "You're saying I need to go back to San Francisco right after the earthquake happens? That's worse than facing the air raids in World War I London!"

Malcolm lifts one eyebrow.

I hate it when he's right. And he's always right.

But is he, really? Would Mom try to keep San Francisco from burning down? I grab the mouse from Malcolm and click on a map in the sidebar. It shows all of downtown, all of Chinatown, everything south of Market, flattened.

If San Francisco hadn't been destroyed, what difference

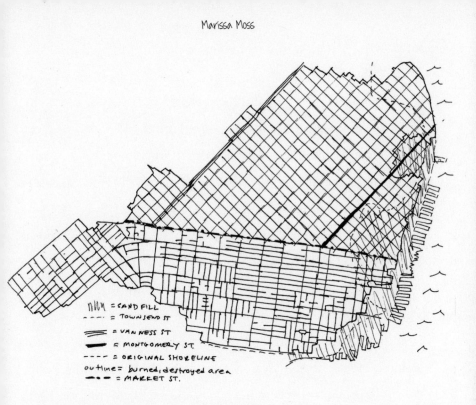

would that have made? Besides saving lives, money, time, hardship. I mean, it's not a question of injustice, is it? The big theme of everything Mom's done so far has been trying to make people more tolerant – of other religions, other beliefs, other cultures, other genders.

So what's the enemy of tolerance?

Suddenly I feel ice cold.

"It's not the earthquake," I whisper. "It's something much, much worse."

"What do you mean?" Malcolm rolls his eyes, ready to say my idea is ridiculous.

"I don't know what needs to change in the past, but I think

I know what Mom's trying to change in our future."

"What?"

"Some awful terrorist attack. Here."

Malcolm snorts. "How do you figure that?"

"Think about it — Mom's been trying to make the world more fair, to stamp out prejudice and narrow-minded thinking throughout the centuries."

Malcolm's quiet. He gets it. What's causing terrorism all over the world lately has been people's beliefs that Western values are corrupting the world, that religious values should triumph over secular ones. In a way, we're going back to the same problems Giordano Bruno faced in 17th century Rome — freedom of thought vs. strict ideologies. Back then it was the Catholic Church telling people they could only think a certain way — or die. Now it's radical Islam.

So if I were a terrorist, what would I try to destroy in San Francisco? Where would I cause the most damage?

"You're thinking of a bomb going off in the Financial District? Something like that?" Malcolm's taking me seriously. That's a huge relief.

"Or maybe on BART. That would be terrifying — an explosion during rush hour." I shudder. I hate the tunnel under the bay as it is. Except I usually worry about an earthquake, not terrorism.

"Don't get all paranoid! And say you're right, Mom's trying to stop an attack. What could she change to do that?" Malcolm shakes his head. "It'd be more helpful to warn the police in our present instead of trying to tip the right domino in the past to make a difference in the future."

"I agree, but she may have already tried that – traveled to our future for just that reason. And failed. Arthur Conan Doyle tried to save his son that way. But he couldn't. That's why he told me only we can change our own futures, in our own present times." Could this really be what Mom wants to change? And can I change it myself at the right time?

Malcolm sighs. "Don't say anything about this to Dad. He's worried enough already."

"Can I do this, Malcolm? Can I get Mom back here? If she would just tell us what the attack will be, maybe we can avoid it. We don't take BART that day, don't go to San Francisco. It seems so preventable, at least for us."

"There must be a reason that won't work or Mom would have already done it. Forget about the future for now. We need to focus on getting her home."

"Okay." I turn back to the earthquake map. "Let's think about this. What long-term change would Mom make if the city didn't burn down that way? How could she prevent terrorism a century or so later?"

"Fewer refugees? Less corruption as the city rebuilt? Maybe the design of the city would be different? If it's not the earthquake, what could it be?" Malcolm starts typing again, sorting through sites so quickly, I can't follow what he's looking at.

The problem is I just don't know enough California history to pick the right time. We've studied the California missions, the Gold Rush, the pioneers, and that's about it. What other history does a young state like California have?

I try to shove away the idea of any kind of attack. I need to clear my head, to calm my heart, which is beating so fast I can hear it pounding in my ears. I leave Malcolm to his lightning research and go where I've gone since I was a little kid and needed a calm, quiet place. I use the maple tree next to the house as a ladder to get onto the roof. We live in the Berkeley hills and the roof is my favorite thinking – or not-thinking – place. From there, you can see three bridges – the Bay Bridge connecting Oakland to San Francisco, the San Rafael bridge connecting Richmond to Marin, and most beautiful of all, the Golden Gate.

It's one of those gorgeous days when the bay looks like glass, San Francisco shimmers as if it's magical, and the white prison of Alcatraz is a slab of cake on a platter. I wouldn't change any of it, not for any reason. I scan the horizon, as if I could see Mom from this distance. Of course I can't, but as my eyes rest on the Golden

Gate, my favorite part of the view, my stomach jolts. Is the bridge a Touchstone? If it is, it would be the biggest Touchstone I've ever seen. Usually they're statues or fountains, things made of stone, maybe bronze.

Dad walks up to the front door, arms full of groceries. I climb down the tree and reach for one of the shopping bags.

"Have you figured out what time you're going to, what Mom is trying to do?" he asks as we walk into the kitchen.

"The 1906 earthquake." Malcolm answers before I can say anything.

"Pretty hard to change Mother Nature," Dad says.

Malcolm gives him the same explanation about dynamite. If he's trying to sound reassuring by not talking about terrorism, he's chosen the wrong tactic. Dad slams down a box of cereal on the counter.

"Absolutely not! Mira's been shoved in jail twice already while time-traveling! I'm not having her face martial law in San Francisco. You know, they shot people on sight. Looters, they said, but no questions were asked, so people carrying their own belongings were killed." Dad grabs the bag of apples out of my hand. "You are NOT going back to 1906, at least not in April. Wait until May, when they start rebuilding. Or forget the earthquake entirely! Pick another date."

"Dad, Mira has to go when Mom is, not when you want her to go."

"You don't know that's when Mom is. You're guessing. We're all guessing!"

That ends the discussion for our first day back in Berkeley. We empty our suitcases, make dinner, and sit down to eat as if it's a regular day. But as soon as the dishes are cleared, Malcolm goes back to his research. And I go back to mine.

Which means lying down on my familiar comforter and closing my eyes. Not because I'm tired, though I'm definitely jet-lagged. My nerves are way too jangled to sleep. But because I want the comfort of my bed. And I want to think some more. Or really, not think, to allow myself just to listen. That's how I get my best ideas. The key is not to focus on anything at all, to let my thoughts go soft and vague.

I'm about to start 8th grade, too big for stuffed animals, but my old teddy bear, fox, and kitty cat still keep me company in bed. The bear has a button sewn on instead of a lost eye and the fox is squashed from the many times I've slept on top of it. I snuggle with

them, feeling as if I could time-travel right there, back to when I was little, opening my eyes to find the drawing kit Mom had set out at the foot of the bed for my fifth birthday. Getting up extra early on the first day of 6th grade, so I could change my clothes three times before finally giving up and wearing a black T-shirt and jeans. I'd been so nervous about starting middle school and here I am about to finish it. With much bigger worries than what to wear!

I tell myself there's nothing to be nervous about. All I have to do is think about Mom. Or not think about her.

Images flit before me. Paris, where I first time-traveled, the gargoyles on Notre Dame, meeting the artist, Edgar Degas, watching him sketch at the race track, walk- ing through Montmartre, seeing  the paintings at the Impressionist show, Monet's beautiful garden at Giverny. Almost kissing Claude, Degas' assistant.

And then a blast of cold shoots through me as I remember

 the first time I saw the Watcher.

I close my eyes tightly, trying to push her away in my mind.

Instead, I picture Rome, where we'd  gone next. Cows grazing in the Forum, the Colosseum, Giovanni and his warm, friendly eyes, the clouds over the Pantheon, the meridian tracking the seasons on the floor of the church. The sun sweeping over the signs of the zodiac set into the marble floor, the lion, the ram, the fishes, then the scales, Mom's sign.

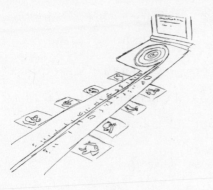

I sit straight up! I've gotten my idea, just like I knew I would – I don't have to pick a time at all. Mom will do that. Just as she always has before. She's told me where to go in the postcards, not when. All I have to do is find a Touchstone and see when it takes me to. Worst come to worst, I can always grab the Touchstone again and get back to now. I'm getting better at reaching home close to the time I leave. Dad and Malcolm might not even know I've gone. And this time, I'll have Mom with me when I come back.

July 15

The crowd of morning commuters has thinned out by the time Dad drops Malcolm and me off at the BART station.

"What if I need your help?" I try not to whine.

"You have a phone, right? I don't need to hold your hand. I can't anyway, once you time-travel. You want your mother to treat you like a responsible person? Well, that's what I'm doing."

I get out of the car. "Fine! Malcolm and I will handle things."

"Of course you will," Dad says. "Besides, I have a meeting with someone from the grant foundation in Marin. They want to suggest other Wonders I should photograph. Call when you get back on BART and I'll pick you up."

"See ya!" Malcolm shuts the door. He seems glad Dad's not coming.

"You don't care that we're on our own?" I ask once we're waiting on the platform for the next San Francisco-bound train.

"I've been thinking about this. It's our future at stake. We're the ones who matter here, so maybe Dad really shouldn't be involved at all." Malcolm tips back on his heels confidently. "I think this is happening the way it's supposed to, with just you and me. This time, finally, it'll work. Together we'll convince Mom to come home."

I'm grateful he used that word – together.

We're getting off at Montgomery station because it seems the most historical. According to Malcolm, Montgomery Street marked the edge of the city in the 1850s. Wharves jutted off the street into the bay. Later the wharves became streets as landfill was dumped between them. Boats that had been docked in water became fixed in earth. Some were used as buildings, like saloons, hotels, even jails. Supposedly the Transamerica Pyramid was built on one of those hulking wrecks.

So that street seems like a good place to look for historical San Francisco. The other choice had been Powell, the cable car turn-around, because that's a bit of living history. But we flipped a coin and heads meant Montgomery.

I've been to Paris, Rome, and London, but stepping out onto Market Street in San Francisco, that familiar bubble of excitement surges through me. It's such a beautiful city, but it's also familiar, friendly. Mine, even if I don't live here.

It's also crowded with tourists. Funny to think that people from all over the world come to visit what's like our backyard (well, front yard).

Malcolm throws open his arms, his new favorite gesture. "Hello, San Francisco!" he bellows.

"Stop that! People will think you're nuts!" I hiss.

But compared to the guys break-dancing, the man preaching the gospel of Save Mother Earth, the young woman with dozens of piercings on her face (facial air conditioning?) begging for spare change, and the cat lady thrusting free kittens at everyone, Malcolm seems sane. I'm glad the naked protestors have picked a different spot today. The last time I saw them, it took weeks to erase those images from inside my eyelids.

"Hey, I'm happy to be here! Aren't you? That's the great thing about living in the Bay Area – you can go all over the world, to all these famous places, but then you come home to this! Imagine going home to Needles, Nevada or Pipetown, Ohio. That's gotta be a huge let-down."

"Okay, we're lucky. Now we've got to figure out a possible Touchstone." I scan down Market Street and up Montgomery. "Usually they're ancient – fountains or statues. What's old here?"

"Isn't the tower at the Ferry building old? Plus I brought a list of old places with me." Malcolm pulls a notebook out of his pocket. So now he's carrying a notebook, too? Maybe I've infected him with my writing habit. Or is he just determined to have some control over what we do? In the present, if not in the past.

Malcolm flips through the pages. "The closest old thing near here is Lotta's Fountain. It's up a couple of blocks, at the corner of Market and Geary. It's still the place where people who survived the Big One gather every April 12th in commemoration."

"The earthquake? You really want me to go back then?"

"It doesn't matter when I want you to go, it's when Mom wants. You said so yourself."

I've noticed this about my brother. When I'm confident,

he's critical of me. When I'm worried, that's when he's encouraging. Why can't he just always be nice?

"If you end up in some time where you don't want to be, you can always find another Touchstone and come back to now."

"That's easy for you to say," I grouse, even though I'd been telling myself exactly the same thing. "If it's hard to find Touchstones now, in modern San Francisco, what will it be like a century or two ago? Will a pile of rocks count as a Touchstone? A ship's anchor?"

"Too bad there aren't portable Touchstones, something you can carry in your pocket. Maybe I'll invent something like that, once I figure out how to make Touchstones."

For some reason, the only things I can carry when I time-travel are my notebook and pen. And while they're useful, comforting even, they're not Touchstones. What if I end up stuck in 1830s San Francisco? Was there even a city then? Probably just the Spanish mission, the one on Dolores Street by the park.

By now we can see what has to be Lotta's Fountain. It's smack in the middle of the sidewalk, but I've never noticed it

before. It doesn't look like a fountain for one thing, more like a bunch of ornamental elements stacked on top of each other. A piece of column, a scrolling bit here, a curlicue there, rosettes and lion heads all mashed together as if the sculptor couldn't make up his mind whether to make a lamppost or a scroll-top desk.

"That's one crazy fountain," Malcolm observes. "Should take you someplace interesting."

"Who was Lotta anyway? Someone who survived the earthquake and built the fountain as a thank you? Or a no, thank you!"

"Oh, this is from before the earthquake, 1875, I think." Malcolm reads from his notebook. "Lotta Crabtree was a child singer-entertainer. She was famous during the Gold Rush. The miners wanted a taste of home comforts and Lotta was a cute kid who could sing and dance. Kids were so rare then, there are stories of miners coming to the city from the mines and paying a lump of gold for the privilege of touching a child or holding a baby. Think of that – gold was more common than children!" Malcolm watches

a mom pushing a toddler in a stroller, while the kid wedges a finger deep into his nose. "I'd take gold any day! Anyway, Lotta made a fortune here and ended up traveling around the country, performing in her own theater company. In the 1880s she was the highest paid actress in America, a really big celebrity. This fountain was her way of thanking San Francisco for starting her career."

It may look like a pile of stuff from someone's attic, but it's definitely a Touchstone. Purple waves shimmer off of its coppery skin. The lions' eyes glow amber, then red, then green.

"Good luck, Mira." Malcolm looks so sure of me, of himself. "I'll be here, waiting for you." He points to a cafe across the street. "Watching this lovely fountain and everyone who comes to touch it. Who knows? Maybe I'll see Mom before you do."

Okay, I know where Malcolm will be and where I'll be. The question is when. I try to clear my head, to think about Mom, only Mom. When it feels right, I reach my hand through the haze of purple, red, and green and touch the fountain. The pavement trembles and splits open, a whoosh of wind spirals around me, constellations spin at dizzying speeds, and the ground pitches under my feet like a rolling wave. A timequake.

July, 1864

When I finally steady myself, the fountain is gone. Panic shoots through me. How will I get back without a Touchstone? I take a deep breath, try to calm down. So much for Malcolm's cheery promise that I could always just come back if I didn't like where I ended up.

Not that I'm in a terrible place. There are no crumbling buildings, no fires. No sign of an earthquake. In fact, I could be in one of those cutesy towns in the Sierra foothills, the ones where you can pan for a gold, and actors wear bonnets and old-fashioned clothes. There aren't any cars, just wagons, and the streets aren't paved, but most of the buildings across the street are three stories high, impressive-looking. Some have the high wooden false fronts you see in old Western movies, but others look more classical, with columns and marble panels. I expect to see a stagecoach rumble past. Or a sheriff's posse galloping by. I can't help thinking of the third *Back to the Future* movie, when Marty McFly ends up back in the Old West. But real life is never like the movies.

I wipe my nervous hands on my skirt. Yes, of course, I'm wearing a dress. No jeans and tennis shoes in this time. At least my clothes are clean and neat, a cheery pink gingham. Now there's a word I've only read because nobody says it. But gingham sounds so much cozier than checkered. And more old-fashioned.

Carts that look like horse-drawn cable cars rumble down the middle of the dirt road. Behind them, a couple of men ride bicycles with giant wheels, the kind you see in old cartoons. There

are a few women carrying parcels, but mostly I see men. Some are elegantly dressed with canes and nice hats, some wear clothes that are so dirty, it's hard to tell what color they are. One man combines both, with fancy epaulets and a hat with an eagle insignia, a tangled beard and stains all over his clothes.

He's riding a bike, which doesn't seem like something a soldier would do. Still, people salute him when he goes by, so he's clearly someone important, despite the rusty bicycle and his need for a shower. Is he somebody I should pay attention to, a hint to why Mom's here?

He turns a corner and is gone before I can get close. If only I could ask Morton, Mom's faithful time-travel friend. But for once there's no sign of him. Nobody to help me at all. At least this place doesn't feel as strange as the other cities I've been to. People speak English – regular American English, not squishy British English that sounds all slanted. And this is a familiar town. It's still San Francisco, after all.

The city isn't as polished as 1880s Paris or 1914 London, but it's not just a collection of miners' tents, either. In fact, looking into the windows of the buildings nearby, I see I've landed in the

middle of the financial district. Not so much banks, but stock brokers' offices. Papers in the windows announce mining stocks bought and sold, silver assessed, U.S. tender bought and sold. (Does tender mean money?) Lumps of gold and silver are displayed next to vials of gold dust, raw lumps of ore with silverish streaks, and fancy brass scales. From all the ads, it's clear that silver matters much more than gold. Stocks in a variety of silver mines are offered, from the Little Bend Mine to the Jackass Hill Mine, the Annipolitan to the Spring Valley. We learned about the Gold Rush in California history, but now the frenzy seems to be all about silver.

I have to figure out what year this is. Clearly before 1875, since the fountain has vanished. I scan the signs in the store windows for any kind of hint. Then I see it – a newspaper left on a window ledge! I unfold the single sheet with the masthead emblazoned *Daily Morning Call* and underneath in small print, July 1, 1864.

1864? I can't think of anything important happening that summer in California. I quickly scan the newspaper for anything momentous. The only thing that strikes me is a short article about an earthquake – not the big one, but another one:

"At five minutes to nine o'clock last night, San Francisco was favored by another earthquake. There were three distinct shocks, two of which were very heavy, and appeared to have been done on purpose, but the third did not amount to much. Here-tofore our earthquakes – as all old citizens experienced in this sort of thing will recollect – have been distinguished by a soothing kind of undulating motion, like the roll of waves on the sea, but we are happy to state that they are shaking her up from below now. The shocks last night came straight up from that direction; and it is sad to reflect, in these spiritual times, that they might possibly have been freighted with urgent messages from some of our departed friends. The suggestion is worthy a moment's serious reflection, at any rate."

It's written more like a joke than a newspaper story. There are no articles about political corruption or injustice, nothing like the piece Emile Zola wrote while I was in Paris.

So I know the date, but I'm no closer to figuring out where Mom might be or what she could be planning.

But somehow I'm not anxious about all that. Probably because this is the most familiar of all the places I've time-traveled to. Not just because I know modern San Francisco, but because I've seen my share of Westerns. I've read *Little House on the Prairie*. I've taken field trips to Sutter's Fort and Old Town Sacramento. I feel like I could walk into one of these general stores and find barrels full of old-fashioned candy, fudge, and popcorn in every flavor imaginable. Just like they have in tourist towns in the Sierra foothills.

Walking down Montgomery (this is still Montgomery Street, right?), I find myself at the edge of the city, just as Malcolm described. There are a few short streets beyond, but then nothing except docks and ships, so many their masts are like a leafless forest.

Looking past them at the water, the horizon is oddly bare. There are no bridges, not one. Without them, the bay is like a toothless mouth.

Still, this is my view, my bay. That's comforting somehow.

I turn back to look at the city, nowhere near as grand as it will become. Sure, there are some nice buildings, faced with stone and a lot of brick, something the modern city avoids because of earthquakes. Guess they didn't know that then. There are also the familiar Victorians, the "painted ladies" of San Francisco. I smile, recognizing parts of present-day San Francisco that are already here.

I've been thinking of the city as a thing for me to study, not a place I'm actually in, so when a young man starts talking to me, I'm as startled as if a character in a book had broken through the page.

"Pardon me, Miss," the red-haired man drawls, holding his hat in both hands. "I'm the reporter for the *Call* and I'm conducting my man-on-the-street interviews, or in this case, girl-on-the-street, a charming little feature introducing different elements of our fair city to our even fairer readers. Such as, where people have come from and what they hope to accomplish here in San Francisco."

I gape at him. He speaks with a soft southern accent, out of place in the Wild West, and he sounds like he's trying to sell me patent medicine.

"You have the look of someone who has only just arrived and that is why I am wondering if you could tell me where you came from and why you chose to brave the arduous journey here?"

How can he tell I've just gotten here? I swallow nervously. "So I look like I don't belong here?" I rasp.

"Have I offended you?" The man's bushy eyebrows shoot up to the top of his forehead. "Usually it takes more than a minute for folks to find me off-putting. Generally several paragraphs are needed, not just a sentence or two."

"No, no, it's fine," I mumble, trying to think of a story to explain myself. He's a reporter, so if anyone can tell me what's going on here, it's him. "I'd love to be part of your feature thing. Can we sit down somewhere? I have some questions for you, too, if you don't mind."

"Weeeeeeeeeeell." He sighs dramatically. "If we sit down,

then I cannot really in all good conscious call it a girl-on-the-street interview anymore." He sighs again, shaking his head. "But my throat is dusty and a drink would be welcome about now. Shall we go to the Cakes & Loaves?"

My stomach grumbles at the mention of cake. I assume he'll be buying, so I nod my head.

The reporter gallantly offers his arm. "May I introduce myself? Sam Clemens of the *Daily Morning Call*."

I need a name quickly, so I use the first one that comes into my head, the same one I used in 1914 London. "Miriam Lodge, pleased to meet you."

For a second I wonder if he's lying, if maybe he's not a reporter at all. But the *Call*? That's the paper I'd just read. And Sam Clemens? The name is familiar somehow.

"Are you the one who wrote about last night's earthquake?" Did I read his name there?

The man smiles broadly. "You are already one of our loyal readers then? And an initiated San Franciscan, since you have enjoyed your first semi-monthly earthquake. We usually expect two per month, you see. In fact, that was part of my salary negotiation – a certain comfortable amount of cash and no more than one earthquake every thirty days. My employer thought I wouldn't notice the second one!"

He's a reporter alright, even though he doesn't talk like any newsman I've ever heard. Instead of the short staccato or heavy dramatic tone of some newspeople, words roll out of his mouth slowly. There's no hurrying them along. Or his pace either. I force myself to amble alongside him. Only the promise of cake keeps me from running circles around him like a small yappy dog. Good thing the restaurant is only a block away or it would have taken us hours to get there. The reporter settles down at one of the small round tables, carefully folding his jacket on a nearby chair. I'm already regretting this. Anything with this man will take forever! It's like being stuck behind a big slow truck on a narrow, windy road.

Still, there'll be cake. When a boy walks over and asks what we'll have, the reporter orders tea, along with raisin buns. For both of us. That's almost as good as cake. The man's a complete stranger, but a full stomach can build a lot of trust. And I want to trust him. There's a warm twinkle to his eyes, as if he's just heard the funniest joke and can't wait to share it with you.

"How long have you written for the *Call?*" I ask.

"Well, now, I have been writing letters as a correspondent for nigh on a year. I was working mostly at the *Territorial Enterprise* in Virginia City. But circumstances beyond my control necessitated leaving Washoe, which brought me to this gentle Paradise." Here the reporter sweeps out his arms, as if the small restaurant is a grand vision of wonder, not a plain wooden room with a few small tables. "Truly, after the dust and grit of Nevada Territory, San Francisco is a pearly gem, a bountiful splendor of a city. And I am now the *Call's* one and only reporter, rather than a sometime correspondent.

Which brings me back to my mission of discovering your intriguing story."

"I don't have an intriguing story," I blurt out, grateful that the boy is back with the tea and buns. Maybe the food will distract the reporter. Where was Washoe, anyway? Was that a nickname for Washington State? Would I look like a total idiot if I asked?

"But you must! A young lady such as yourself, traveling alone? That's a story right there. You have uncommon nerve to face the hazards of the stagecoach or the perils of the steamship, however you made your way here."

Ugh! How do I deal with being a girl at a time when that's not an easy thing to be? In 17th century Rome, I'd dressed as a boy for exactly that reason. I tug at my hair, wishing I'd cut it. Maybe it's not too late. Maybe I can find some overalls some-  where. As soon as I ditch the reporter.

"My brother brought me here on our horse, Bart. He dropped me off." That's almost true.

"He left you here by yourself?" The reporter frowns. "My mama would never allow such behavior! Nor would my sister. And she's someone you don't want to anger!"

I'm digging myself into a deeper hole every time I open my mouth.

"I'm fine. My brother's not far." I shove a chunk of bun into my mouth, chewing noisily. I can't talk while I eat, right?

"You certainly look like a capable young lady. That raisin bun knows to take you very seriously indeed."

Lies are easier to remember if they're close to the truth, so I see what I can come up with that sounds believable. "My father sent me here to look for my mother. She's setting up a home for us while my father pans for gold. My brother's getting supplies but we'll meet up later to head back."

"Are you saying your brother left you in this city alone while he's off on some errands?" Clemens shakes his head. "I can't say I care much for your brother's character. Or his common sense."

"But he's thinks I'm with my mother, not alone."

"Well, now that's a horse of a different color. I misunderstood you. I thought you were looking for your mother, but you're staying with her."

He's more of a reporter than I thought, like a dog with a bone that he won't let go of. Just because he talks slowly doesn't mean he isn't smart. Or stubborn.

"No, not exactly," I try again. "I don't know where my mother is yet. But I will. Soon."

"So your brother left you to find her, not knowing whether you would be successful in your venture or not? I know that brothers can treat their brothers like that – mine certainly has. But sisters, well, they deserve special care and they usually won't let you forget that."

"I thought the West was a place where girls and women could do things they couldn't do back East! That I'd have more freedom here! That's what everyone says in the foothills!" I made that part up, but if they aren't saying it, they should. "I told my brother I could take care of myself. And I can!"

"I can see that now!" Clemens leans back as if my words have pushed him. "I've met many capable women in this fair city and I'm delighted to meet another one today. As will my readers be, I'm sure."

"I've answered your questions. Now it's your turn to answer mine." I take a calming sip of tea. It's not the reporter's fault he's got a dinosaur's view of women. It is 1864 after all. "You must know this city well. Perhaps you could tell me where a lady by herself could find a quiet place to stay? Perhaps you've even seen her around – her name is Serena Goldin Lodge." I give her real last name, along with my fake one. Just in case, I take out my notebook and hold it out to Mr. Clemens.

"She looks like this. I'm not a great artist, but this gives you an idea."

"I would say you draw quite well. Certainly better than my scribbled attempts. The last time I tried to draw a mule, he was so insulted by my portrait, he ate the paper." He leans closer, inspecting the sketch.

I hold my breath. Could it be that easy? Could I run into somebody who knows Mom right away?

"Noooooo." He draws out the word even longer than his usual drawl. "I do not think so. But if she is a lady of quality and has the means, she would stay at Lick House. I would, if I could afford it!"

I'm not sure how much money Mom would have in this time, but in the past, she'd tended to stay in government offices. More protected, maybe. "Where else?"

"There is the Russ House, the Grand." He pauses, longer than his usual gaps between words. "And for those of more meager, yet still comfortable means, there is always the Occidental. Which is where I stay on my generous reporter's salary."

I jot down the names, glancing at the empty plate where the buns used to be, wishing some more would magically appear. "I didn't realize there were so many hotels already."

"Already?"

"I mean," I catch myself, "wasn't San Francisco just a dot on the map until the Gold Rush? So all these places must have been built in the last decade."

"True enough." Clemens nods. "I have heard how folks would sleep practically on top of each other in the '50s. There was nothing here except tents and lean-tos, quickly cobbled-together sheds. And look at her now! Isn't she grand?" He gestures toward the plate glass window at the bank across the street.

I'm not sure "grand" is the word I'd use. Nice enough, I suppose.

"Do you mind giving me some addresses?"

The reporter chuckles. "Who is doing the interviewing here? And you even have a reporter's notebook. Have you done this before?"

I feel my cheeks go hot. "I told you my story isn't interesting. But you may as well help me. I mean, once I find my mother, maybe she can tell you her story." It's a lame offer. "Or I could help you in another way." Though I have no idea how.

One of his bushy eyebrows shoots up again. Is he actually considering what I could do?

"The Grand is closest, on Montgomery near here. Keep walking down Montgomery and you find the Lick House, at Sutter. The Occidental is just a bit further down, between Sutter and Bush. And then there is the Russ House on the corner of Pine. Follow Montgomery and you find them all."

"Anything else, sir?" The boy asks, collecting our empty plates.

"I think that will do, Sandy." The reporter makes no move to pay.

I gulp. Does he expect me to treat him? He'd suggested getting something to eat, so shouldn't he pay? Plus he's a grown up with a job. Except, of course, the waiter is even younger than me, so there's no reason not to expect me to have cash.

"Um, I guess I should be going," I say, hoping that's hint enough for Clemens to pull out his wallet.

"Not so fast, surely!"

"But I don't have any money!" I blurt out, my face feeling redder than ever.

The reporter throws back his head and laughs, a rollicking roll of laughter that flusters me even more.

I want to bolt out of there, but what if he calls me a thief and has me thrown into jail? I'd had enough of that in London and Rome.

Finally Clemens' laugh sputters out. He leans forward, fixing his bright blue eyes on me. "I did not mean to suggest that you should pay! You just gave me an idea when you suggested you could do something for me. And now, hearing that you are short of funds, I think you will find my proposition most welcome."

I brace myself for the suggestion that I clean his room or do his laundry.

"It sounds like you need work. I happen to have a surplus of that commodity. Which means I rise first thing in the morning to head to the courts and police station to collect the news there, walk all over the city during the day, searching for stories such as yours, spend my nights at every single show in town in order to file reviews. I am not back in my bed until well after midnight with all I have to cover!"

For somebody with so much to do, he doesn't seem in much of a hurry to do any of it.

"Of course, I wouldn't ask you to do anything improper. You wouldn't write up the crime reports. Those are my favorites in any case. They're often the most entertaining scraps of the day, far more full of intrigue and drama than the theater. Ah, the theater, that could be just the ticket! I've seen more proclamations of love, patriotism, and holy righteousness than I care to recall. At this point, they all blur together into a single stream of nonsense. You are young and fresh and eager. You have a notebook already. You know how to ask questions."

"You mean you'd pay me to see shows and write about them?" I can't believe my luck!

"You are eminently qualified. You can read and write, which is more than most folks can say, and I desperately need an assistant. Instead of reviewing comedies, tragedies, and musical scenarios, I could play cards and enjoy a late supper. What do you say?"

A job as a reporter? In my real time, nobody would hire me to do anything except babysit. Sometimes the past was actually better. Even for a girl.

Clemens stands up and puts on his jacket. "How about you come along with me for the next few days? You can be my shadow, see what I do and then we can figure out which things fit you best. Though the theater is definitely yours. Without a relaxed meal and postprandial cigar, my mind stutters and shuffles. I am the kind of man who needs some leisure to write his best."

He seems like the kind of man who needs leisure period.

"That sounds perfect!" I can't stop grinning. Except there's still the awkward problem of payment. "Ahem," I murmur, staring at my shoes. "The bill?"

"Don't you worry about that! Sandy knows to put it on my tab, don't you, Sandy?"

"Yessir!" the boy calls from the back, among the clattering dishes.

I'm practically dancing as we head down Montgomery Street. Even without any kind of hint from Mom, I've found a job. With that, it'll be easy to get a room somewhere. Plus I've met someone who can really help me. Who knows more about a city and what's going on than the local reporter?

We turn down Commercial Street and Clemens points out the *Call* offices. They're in the same brick building as the U.S. Mint. News made in one place, money made in the other. They both use printing presses, so it makes sense.

Clemens opens the front door and ushers me upstairs to the third floor. The printing press, a big, hulking machine, takes up most of the space. Next to it is a long table covered with wooden boxes full of metal letters. There are a couple of desks, one big and one small, a few chairs, a wooden filing cabinet, and not much else. Just one boy, a little older than me, sweeping paper cuttings on the floor.

"This is where you will file all your reports. Journalism is an honorable profession, one that teaches you not to waste a single word, to stick to the facts and nothing but the facts." Clemens says this with such a broad smile, I get the feeling he's having a joke at my expense. "Our typesetter and my good friend, Steve Gillis, seems to be away, but this young fellow is Scout Hutchins. Steve has his assistant and now I have mine. Scout, this is Miriam Lodge, newly arrived to our fair city and eager to enter the distinguished world of journalistic enterprise."

Scout sets down the broom and comes forward to shake my hand.

His fingers feel warm and familiar. And his face? I look closer and am jolted by a deep sense of recognition. I know this boy. But how?

"Pleased to meet you, Miss Miriam." Scout's lopsided smile sets my heart racing. The forehead is broader and the eyes green now, but it's him somehow. Claude, the artist apprentice I almost kissed in Paris, Giovanni, the Roman servant from the 1600s, and Clark, the boy from the Underground in World War I London. Somehow they're all related.

"In San Francisco, it is our quaint custom to shake hands for several seconds. Not for several minutes. Certainly not for half an hour." Clemens folds his arms and leans against the wall. Waiting.

"Oh, of course, pardon me!" I drop Scout's hand, suddenly all too aware I've been gripping it tightly for who knows how long. "It's just that you remind me of someone."

"A friend, I should hope." Scout smiles again. And my heart melts even more.

"I hope so, too. I mean, I hope we can be friends," I babble.

"This is all very charming, I'm sure, but shall we leave the friendship for later? I wanted to show Miss Lodge where she should file her stories." Clemens points to the biggest desk in the room, the one that looks like an old-fashioned teacher's desk made of heavy, dark wood. "And of course, you are welcome to write them here, if you like."

Working here now has a definite added attraction – Scout. I nod and try to look like a reporter, serious and smart. "What show do you want me to see tonight?"

"Show? You mean shows! This is San Francisco, where a new revue – or two or three – opens every night! You have to go to several of them, so you'll just have time to duck your head in, note down the essentials, ask someone from the audience for a quick opinion, then move on to the next. When you have enough to write about each one, you get to work, summing up the delights and disasters of each performer, the quality of the audience, the charms or lack thereof in each production. That all has to be submitted tonight (or very early tomorrow morning), so it can be set in the next day's paper. You cannot wait until morning to write – that would be far too late."

I gulp. That's more work than I bargained for. And what if Clemens asks me to write a sample for him on the spot?

"This is not great literature you'll be writing," Clemens reassures me. "Just enough words to fill the acreage of the paper and satisfy the boss, Mr. Barnes. He's always telling me not to embellish, to eschew all adjectives, adverbs, and flowery phrases. Mr. Barnes is a verb and noun man, in that order. More verbs are fine. Fewer nouns are as well. If I could write a story using only verbs, he would be a happy man indeed."

"But won't I need adjectives to describe plays? Aren't I supposed to say if they're good or bad?"

"If you feel so moved, but brief descriptions of the plot and the actors will suffice. If there are discounts or cheap seats, that would be most newsworthy. But the main thing is to fill the column with ink. And now, shall we head to the police station? That's my first stop of the morning, to find out who has been arrested over-night. It usually provides fodder for several inches of newsprint."

Back out on the street, Clemens points out the assaying companies, the banks, the office for another newspaper, the *Alta Californian*. "This here is called the Monkey Block, the commercial and literary heart of the city. My editor may keep my sentences short, but Bret Harte, neighborly employee at the U.S. Mint, occasional writer, and also editor at

the *Californian,* delights in long, rollicking sentences. Why, some of his go on for pages, all lovely curlicues and picturesque metaphors, but once you've finished reading them, you have no idea what he's actually said."

"Why don't you write for him then? It sounds like a better fit for your style."

"If he paid as generously as the *Call,* I would. But a man must eat. Lofty ideals and artistic passion don't normally provide much in the way of sustenance. I may be an idealist, but my stomach is a realist."

"Too bad you can't have both – writing the way you want for the money you want."

"That's the conundrum of the world! If you could solve that one, writers throughout the ages would revere you as genius."

I can't shake the nagging feeling that the name Sam Clemens is familiar. Is he a writer I should know? Is Bret Harte? If only I could ask Malcolm!

We get to the police station, part of the big City Hall building at Pacific and Montgomery. It's weird seeing San Francisco like this. The Monkey Block looked like it was right where the big Transamerica Pyramid stands now and this dirt road would become the heart of the modern financial district. I feel like I'm seeing the city in layers, the way archeologists must feel when they dig down and discover cities on top of cities.

Mira's Diary: California Dreaming

"Before we go in, I should warn you that the average police officer is big and powerful with no particular mental skills, so I try not to waste time talking to them. They'll give you the barest of information, some of it completely false. The detectives are something else entirely. They have incredible instincts and can discern clues where others see nothing of particular interest. I've seen Detective Rose pick up a chicken's tail feather on Montgomery Street and tell in a moment what roost it came from in the Mission. If the theft is recent, he can smell the premises and tell which block in Sacramento Street the man lives in who committed it, by some exquisite difference in the stink left behind which he knows to be peculiar to one particular block of buildings. Then there's Detective Piper who finds a cake, dropped in the Lick House by a thief, and sits down to read it as another man would a newspaper. It informs him who baked the cake, who bought it, where the purchaser lives. Then Piper marches away two miles to the Presidio, grabs the thief, confronts him with the cake that cannot lie, makes him shed his boots and finds $200 in greenbacks in them. Not finished, however, the determined detective then makes the thief shuck off his coat and discovers upon him an additional store of stolen gold."

That sounds like a tall tale, if ever I've heard one. Do I need to worry that one of these detectives can sniff out that I'm from a different time? Or is Clemens just caught up in telling a good story?

"You're keeping the police station beat, aren't you? I don't need to know this, do I?" I try not to sound nervous, to tamp down the pinched squeak in my voice.

"I would think you would want to know about this, whether you have to cover the problems of law and order or simply review entertainments. Reporters should be curious. They should ask a lot of questions, all the hows, whys, and whatfors. When we first met, questions fairly tripped off your tongue, which I took as a good trait for a journalist, well, for a human being, really."

I'm curious, but I don't want the police to be. Or the reporter.

"After you, Mr. Clemens." I pull open the heavy door. I can't help it, I want him to like me. "You'll see, I'm eager to hear all about last night's crimes."

Once inside though, I doubt I'll impress the reporter. I can't even tell who's a regular policeman and who's a detective. The men all wear helmets like British bobbies, with big brass buttons down the front of their coats, and they all have bushy mustaches. They look like Keystone Cops and I almost expect them to start throwing pies in each other's faces. It's hard to take them seriously.

Then I remember the silly-looking police in 1914 London and how they almost shoved me in jail. I wipe the smile off my face and try to look like a reporter digging for news.

"No detectives here, I see." Mr. Clemens winks at me. "So

what stories can I possibly write about? Any interesting adventures last night or early this morning?"

"You tell me." One of the policemen yawns and hands Mr. Clemens a list.

"Now this looks interesting. Some woman accosted a fruit-and-vegetable seller. Was she accusing him of cheating her with rotten tomatoes or moldy cucumbers? Did you arrest her?"

"I was gonna," says the officer. "But it didn't seem worth the trouble, her being a lady and all. I just gave her a stern warning, I did. But the vegetable fellow, he wanted her to pay up. She tipped over his cart, see, setting carrots, onions, and apples rolling down the street."

"You're right, hardly seems worth writing down. But it might add a spot of color. I could have fun with it – felonious fruit or vicious vegetable mayhem! What do you think?" Mr. Clemens turns to me. "Seeing as there's no detective to regale us with finding buried treasure or sniffing out a thief from a shoe print."

"Doesn't seem like much of a crime. Or a story." I'm as disappointed as Clemens clearly is. Nothing dramatic or fun to start our day with.

"With my editor, that hardly matters. But I do need names. Facts are given far too much value in my opinion, but it doesn't hurt to salt a few of them in every article, just enough to give a story spice." Clemens takes a notebook out of his pocket, not that different from my own, and starts writing. "Malka Fischer was the assailant and the merchant was Luigi Giannini. The names alone provide a lot of color and I'm sure I can find something clever to say about fishing for fruit."

Malka Fischer? That's Mom's great-great-(another great?) grandmother! Only she should still be in Lithuania in the 1860s, not in San Francisco. It has to be Mom, using Malka's name! But why would she attack a vegetable peddler?

"You're sure that's her name?" I try to see the police report. "Did you write down her address?"

"Now calm down, little missy! What business is this of yours?" the policeman growls. "Mr. Clemens I know. He stands me a pint now and then. What have you done for me? Why are you even here?"

"Please forgive her." Clemens smiles. "She's a new apprentice and doesn't understand the ins and outs of police procedure. She hasn't learned the intricate balances justice and journalism demand."

"Yes, I'm sorry," I say, feeling not one bit sorry. "I was just hoping for a bigger story. Sir."

"This isn't our lucky day, it seems. Usually there's something more serious than fruit dumping to write about. But if this is what we have, we'll make apple cider from apples." Mr. Clemens finishes his notes and hands the report back to the officer.

We walk out of the building in silence which I already know isn't normal for Clemens. I'm almost afraid to ask him, but we've only gone a few feet when I can't take it anymore.

"Did you write down the address? Seems like a useful fact."

Clemens takes the notebook out of his pocket and hands it to me. "You mean the address of one Malka Fischer, someone you clearly know and care about. Not your mother, but an aunt perhaps, a close friend?"

"Yes, thank you so much! She's someone I know from home and she can tell me where to find my mother. How about we go talk to her together? She can give us her side of the story. Maybe the vegetable seller tried to cheat her."

"I'll pass on the interview, but I can see you won't be much use until you've found her, so you go on ahead. But come back to the *Call* as soon as you're done. I'll put together a list of the shows you need to see tonight."

I babble my thanks and turn back down Montgomery. It seems like the entire city is on this street or just a few blocks off it. The address isn't far and turns out to be a plain wooden house, not a hotel at all, though a sign in the window advertises rooms to let for 50 cents a night.

I wipe the sweat off my face, try to calm my thundering heart, and knock on the door. Please be home, Mom, please, I pray.

A short dumpling of a woman opens the door. "Yes?" Her face is red and chapped like it's been scrubbed

too much, her eyes small blue marbles in the dough of her skin. But the smile is friendly.

"I'm looking for Malka Fischer. I believe she rents from you."

"Mrs. Fischer? Of course. Upstairs, third door on the right." The woman opens the door wider and points to the stairs behind her.

Now I just have to think of some way to get Mom to listen to me, not bolt the way she always does. Actually, I have the advantage this time. What's she going to do, climb out the window?

I stand in front of the door, sweat pouring off of me as I search for the magic words to convince her to come home with me. I can only think of four. So I straighten myself up and knock on the door.

"Come in," a muffled voice calls out.

I turn the knob, hurl myself in, and close the door behind me. Before Mom can say anything, I blurt out, "Mom, I love you!"

The room is plain, with only a bed and a small table below the narrow window. Too small to jump out of, I notice. The woman seated at the table stands up and turns around.

Only it isn't Mom.

It's the Watcher.

"What are you doing here? Why are you calling yourself Malka Fischer?" The

disappointment is so deep, I feel sick to my stomach.

"You know why I'm here. The same reason you are. Or should be – to stop your mother."

"Then why use that name?"

"Why not?" The Watcher smiles, but she's not being friendly. I almost expect to see fangs. "I'll take what I can from her. And it won't just be her name."

"Leave her alone! Leave us alone! I told you I'd convince her to come home. You don't need to punish her!"

"She's breaking the rules. You know what happens to people like her."

Actually, I don't, not exactly, but I'm too afraid to ask. It's enough knowing that the Watcher arranged for Giordano Bruno's awful death. And for Emile Zola's. Mom can't be next!

The Watcher blinks slowly. She's always reminded me of a snake, for all her beauty.

"So if you know where your mother is, tell me now. No sense in dragging all this out longer than necessary. You're just risking her making another change that shouldn't happen."

"I have no idea where she is and if I did, I wouldn't tell you!"

The Watcher grabs my wrist, holding it in a tight vise. "Yes, you would. I'd make you!"

I want to pull my arm back, but the Watcher's grip is steely strong. Instead, I force my mouth into my own fake smile. "Good thing I don't know anything then."

The Watcher lets go, her face smoldering. "You're useless, totally useless! Your mother is a criminal. And you, you're just a fool!"

I can't get out of the room fast enough. Mom may be bending the rules, but she's not a criminal! I run down the stairs, holding up my skirt clumsily. Why can't I wear jeans in the past – and some decent running shoes? I bolt out the front door, ignoring the landlady's confused stare.

I'm almost back at the *Call* offices when I realize I should have asked the Watcher about the vegetable cart. Why tip it over? Is there some connection between Mom and the vegetable seller? But she'd probably lie to me anyway. I wonder if she's ever told me the truth. Was she really enforcing the time-travel rules or did she have a personal grudge against Mom? It sure felt personal.

Clemens isn't in the office, but Scout is. I must look a horrible mess, because he offers me a glass of water right away.

"Seems like you've had a bit of a shock, miss."

His tone is so kind and gentle, I burst into tears. It's stupid, but I can't stop. All the tension and fear pours out of me in big, wracking sobs. I have to give him credit – he doesn't run away, though he looks like he wishes he could. I blow my nose on the handkerchief he hands me, wipe the wetness from my face.

"I'm sorry," I say once I've finally stopped crying. "This is silly. It's just that I ran into someone I'd rather not see and I still haven't found my mother." Scout feels like a close friend, someone I can trust, someone I already have trusted. But there's no way he'll ever kiss me the way Claude almost did, the way Giovanni and Clark wanted to, not now that he's seen me red-nosed and blubbering.

Anyway, that's for the best. He can be a friend, that's all. Claude taught me that. And having a friend matters – a lot!

"Maybe I can help you find your mother. Have you tried the rooming houses? I can go with you, if you like."

I look at him gratefully. "Yes, that would be nice."

Scout takes off the leather apron he's been wearing. "How about now? I can take a break for an hour or so."

We go from hotel to hotel, but there's nobody answering Mom's name or description at any of them. As we walk, I ask Scout questions about the news, what's happening in San Francisco these days, hoping for a clue about what Mom wants to change.

"So tell me some of Mr. Clemens' big scoops, the major stories he's written about."

"He writes a lot about shows, the things you'll be doing. He's partial to Lotta Crabtree. She's been the Sweetheart of San Francisco since she was twelve years old. Started performing when she was only six! I've seen her sing and dance and play the banjo. She's mighty fine."

Lotta Crabtree? She was the person who put up the fountain, the Touchstone that got me here. That has to mean something.

Maybe she's involved in the thing Mom wants to change.

"Where is she performing now? Will I see her tonight?" I scan the notices outside the theater we're passing.

"Oh, no, we're too small for her now. She left for New York earlier this year. She'll be a national star before you know it!"

So the fountain doesn't mean anything. Still, maybe reviewing these shows

will be more useful than I expected. There still might be some connection.

"Any other big stories?" I press.

"Big? For the *Call?*" Scout shrugs. "You're not supposed to write about politics or anything that can put someone's nose out of joint. It's not that kind of newspaper. Anyway, what I like is the way Mr. Clemens writes his stories. Mr. Barnes doesn't like his 'style,' as he calls it, but I do. When you read 'em, it's like he's talking to you, like you're snug around a fire."

I can't say I felt that from the earthquake story. It wasn't exactly cozy, but I think I see what Scout means. There's a tone to what Clemens writes that doesn't sound like dry newspaper reporting. Which is probably exactly what the editor doesn't like. But none of this helps me find Mom. Plus I'm hungry and tired. I may have a job, but I don't have any money yet.

Scout shoots me a look, as if he can hear my stomach grumbling. And maybe he can.

"We can stop for lunch at a saloon," he suggests. "A free lunch. You can get a big spread. It's the way most folks in town eat."

I thought there's no such thing as a free lunch! "Really?" I say. "Why free? What's the catch?" And did he really say "saloon?" Am I in the Wild West or in 1864 San Francisco? I don't see any cowboys or tumbleweeds. Just people going to work, running errands. Horse-drawn carts and wagons fill the streets with their reassuring clip-clop sounds.

"You pay for drinks and get free food. A glass of lemonade is a nickel and with it, you get all you can eat. Course, most fellas end up drinking a lot of beer, but I'm careful. You can go in, so long as you're with me."

"I couldn't go by myself?"

"Most ladies wouldn't go to such establishments on their own," Scout explains as if that's totally obvious.

So I'm not sure what to expect when he leads me into The Harquette Brothers' Palace of Art Saloon and Restaurant. It doesn't have the swinging doors you see in westerns, but then with a snooty name like "Palace of Art," I guess it wouldn't. The place can't make up its mind what it wants to be – saloon or restaurant. But once inside, it's clear where the name comes from. The walls are covered with paintings. Small marble sculptures and big silver cups are displayed on pedestals. Along one side of the room is a bar, along the other a long counter full of different dishes. People sit at tables and order regular meals as well, both men and women, so I don't feel completely out of place.

Five cents isn't much, but I don't even have that. I'll get paid eventually, so my growling stomach gives me the courage to ask Scout for a loan.

"Sure," he says, thumping a dime down on the bar. "Two lemonades," he orders and leaves me to wait for the glasses while he heads over to the buffet.

He comes back with a menu and a plate piled high with food. "Here are the choices, if you want to know the names of things. I just care how it tastes, not what it's called."

Looking at his plate, I can see what he means. I recognize a slice of ham and some pork and beans. There are crackers, cheese,

and smoked salmon. And then there's a lot of stuff I don't know. I scan the menu and even reading the words, I have no idea what half of these things are. I guess San Francisco was really into food, even back in the 1860s!

I copy the list into my notebook. Malcolm will want to know exactly what a gold miner would eat.

Radishes, crab salad, celery, clam juice, Bolinas Bay clams, head cheese, pig's head, saucisses a la famille, beef a la Chile Colorado, chili con carne, Honolulu beans, chicken croquette, veal croquette, terrapin stew, fried clams, sardines, boiled ham, apples, corned beef, cold tongue, beef stew, pork and beans, chipped beef, smoked salmon, cheese, crackers, cracked crab, Holland herring, almonds, popcorn, and Saratoga chips. (These last turn out to be regular potato chips, despite the fancy name.)

What a mouthful! And stomachful! The other side of the menu lists the paid lunch, which includes a drink, all for twenty-five cents. There are some of the same dishes, but there's a lot less choice on the paid menu. So why would anyone pay?

"I don't get this." I sit down next to Scout with my own full plate. I'm willing to try new things, but draw the line at head cheese, pig's head, terrapin stew, and cold tongue (you can actually see the bumps on the tongue like pimply meat!). Those are all too gross to even look at, much less taste. "Why would anyone buy the other lunch?"

"Most people don't. They take the free lunch and end up drinking more than what the paid lunch would cost. There are a lot of salty foods here, things to make you thirsty, so better sip that lemonade or it'll be costing you double."

I make myself chew slowly, trying not to rudely bolt down my food. It's all better than good – it's delicious. I can't help smiling. I think of my favorite San Francisco foods, like sourdough bread, Dungeness crab and Ghirardelli chocolate. For all its rough beginnings, the city got food right pretty quickly.

"Now I just need a cheap place to stay." I tell Scout. "Any ideas? Maybe I could sleep in the newspaper office?"

"That's not for a proper young lady! You need a rooming house. I have a place in Chinatown that's not bad. It's near where Mr. Clemens stays, which is another possibility."

"But I don't have any money yet. It's one thing to borrow a nickel for lunch. A room is going to cost a lot more, right? Will someone rent a room without payment in advance?"

"I'm sure Mr. Clemens will lend you the money. He's gonna pay you and he doesn't want you sleeping on the street. Maybe you'll find your mother before it gets dark. That'd be the best thing."

Yeah, it would. If I found Mom, I could get out of here and wouldn't need to worry about a room or meals or money. So after lunch, Scout goes back to the *Call* and I spend hours walking all over the city, checking out the hotels and rooming houses we missed. There's no Serena Goldin at any of them and nobody recognizes the sketch I show.

I find my way back to the *Call* building. Good thing San Francisco is so small. You can tramp all over and not get lost. If the bridges were here it would be even easier – the Golden Gate points north and the Bay Bridge points east.

"Any luck?" Scout asks.

I shake my head, discouraged. "Nothing! I still need a place to stay."

Clemens bounces into the office behind me. "We'll take care of that, I assure you! Today has been a good day for news. A host of generals with impressive uniforms and even more impressive mustaches came to inspect the fortifications, from Fort Point to Alcatraces. Shells were fired in magnificent displays of military skill. A brass band played stirring music and chicken salad was served. Best of all, I have sufficient notes to stretch the account to five meaty paragraphs – now there's a newspaper story with heft!"

I'm guessing Alcatraces means Alcatraz, since I know from our fourth-grade class field trip that there was an army fort there long before it became a prison. But that's all I get from Clemens' glowing description.

"Ah, I see you're too troubled by your housing woes to properly admire the shape of this magnificent article. Let's get you settled into a room and then you'll be able to enjoy the theater tonight. Since I have such a substantial story, you won't have to write as much. The paper will be filled with the glories of General McDowell and a host of other impressive names and ranks and mustaches."

Clemens leaves a pile of notes on the desk and ushers me out. He's walking more quickly now, almost at a normal pace, puffing on a cigar as we walk down streets that get more and more crowded, noisy and jostling.

I'm tempted to tell him he shouldn't smoke, that it's bad for him, but that would sound stupid. And be messing with history. Still, I can't help waving the cigar smoke away from me. It's so nasty smelling.

"Does my smoking offend you?" Clemens asks. "I know a gentleman shouldn't smoke around a lady and normally I would restrain myself, but as we're outside, I thought perhaps you would allow me the pleasure of a good cigar."

There's no way to say no without sounding like a whiner. So I lie. "I don't mind at all, go right ahead."

Clemens shifts the cigar to the other side of his mouth, away from me. "Very kind of you. In any case, I'm wagering that soon other odors will overpower the faint aroma from my little cigar. You may even find yourself missing the time when that was all you smelled."

He's right about that. We're in Chinatown soon, not the modern touristy neighborhood with the giant dim sum restaurants

and souvenir shops. Strange, strong smells waft out of doorways and windows. Men and women carry baskets that hang from poles balanced on their shoulders. The men have long braids down their backs and black silk hats, like extra big yarmulkes. The women wear loose tops with pants, and I feel a pang of envy. Lucky them – they don't have to deal with awkward skirts! Most exotic of all, children play in the streets and in the doorways of stores. While the grown-ups wear dark clothes, the kids have on bright colors, some with

fancy embroidery. One pudgy little boy points at me, giggling. I wave at him. A lot of things are different when I time-travel, but little kids stay the same, their curious eyes full of wonder.

Barrels filled with unidentifiable herbs, dried fish, and vegetables line the storefronts. Dead ducks that have been pressed flat

hang in windows like kites on display. I glance into one dark doorway and see men lying on cushions smoking long ceramic pipes.
Could that be an opium den? The thick smoke is sickly sweet and I
quickly cover my nose and hurry away.

Clemens keeps up his
usual steady patter, describing
how one place features the best
noodles, another houses an un-
commonly large pig that keeps
the street clean, and another,
yes, this one with the black
lacquer door, rents cheap
rooms.

I stop, stunned. I'm going to stay here?

"I fear that you don't approve of these lodgings, but I assure
you Mrs. Gee runs a clean, quiet house. I can testify personally to
that, as this is where Steve Gillis and I board."

"Here? I thought you were at the Occidental."

"Ahem." Clemens coughs awkwardly. "I was at the Occidental.
But these rooms are more affordable – and most comfortable!"

No wonder I didn't find Mom at any of the hotels. She's
probably staying someplace like this. A door in a house on a busy
street with no way to know there are rooms for rent.

Anyway, if Clemens stays here, I'm sure it's fine. And he's
right, cheap is what matters most.

Mrs. Gee, a tiny woman with friendly eyes, shows me my room. It's small, but clean, like Clemens said. Better than sleeping in the kitchen, the way I did in Rome. I'm given a key and just like that, I'm set.

I slip the key into my pocket. It's heavy and made of metal, not like the flimsy plastic cards you get at modern hotels. I've never rented my own room before. With its own key. Such a small thing, but it makes me feel big.

"Where's your luggage?" Clemens asks. "Well, you can worry about that later. I need to interview a certain chef about a unique dish he's developing to stir the more refined San Francisco palate. He says it involves Bolinas Bay clams and plenty of garlic. I'll definitely need to taste it."

"What about me? How will I know what theaters to go to? What I should write about?"

As we head back to the *Call,* through streets that get broader and less crowded the further we get from Chinatown, Clemens gives me a quick rundown on the different theaters (well, quick for him with his leisurely drawl). I scribble notes as I walk, jotting down what people want to read about, such as which important people showed up where. And what jewels they wore. As if I can identify precious stones! Or important people!

"The details don't really matter." Clemens reassures me. "I've used the same description of glittering tiaras, diamond- draped throats, lace ruffles, satin flounces, silk bows, and velvet sleeves over and over again. I mix up the order a bit, but the ingredients remain the same. What people want to know is that great elegance and taste displayed itself as much in the audience as on stage. People come to be seen as much as to be entertained."

We walk past a couple of the theaters, so now I know where to go. One theater is by the wharves, the area called the Barbary Coast.

"Perhaps not a place you should venture by yourself. Take Scout with you for that one. Or do what I do – invent the whole thing. In a pinch that will work."

That's like lying for a book report, saying you've read something when you haven't. I've never done that before, despite all the lying I have to do when I time-travel.

"You're new to this, so the spectacles may even entertain you. I've done far too many of them. The plays are melodramatic or sentimental or both. The audience is preening and vain or rowdy and calamitous. That's not the kind of story I want to write about."

"What do you want to write about? Scout tells me you have to avoid politics." I still think it's funny that a newspaper would avoid the exact topic that fills so much media.

"I'm fine with staying far away from that noxious sphere! I'm much more interested in regular folk. The fellows I worked with in the silver mines, the speculators and tradesmen, the adventurers and risk-takers. That's why I started my 'man-on-the-street' feature, the story you were supposed to provide me. But never did, if I may remind you. Ah, well, another slot I need to fill with ink. Which means I should get started on my story, the one about the impressive military mustaches and their shiny-buttoned uniforms, the one that will take up an astonishing amount of space."

Clemens nods at the man working next to Scout as we walk into the newspaper office. He has on an inky apron and is bent over rows of type, so I'm guessing he's the famous Steve Gillis. But Clemens doesn't introduce me and I feel silly just standing there, so I hold out my hand.

"I'm Miriam Lodge, Mr. Clemens' new assistant. You must be Steve Gillis."

"I must be!" Gillis is short and wiry and has an impish smile. I like him right away. He talks twice as fast as Clemens, his movements quick and sure. They're like opposites!

"And I must get to writing!" Clemens says. He settles himself at the desk, takes out his notes and starts pounding on the typewriter, pecking away with two fingers in such an awkward way,

it's painful to watch.

"What do you want me to do?" I ask. "I could type for you if you want to dictate."

Clemens stares at me as if I just suggested walking on the ceiling. "Why would you type instead of me?"

"Because I'm faster."

Scout and Gillis both turn to gape at me. What did I say that's so strange?

"By all means, show me your prowess!" Clemens gets up. "Although I've never dictated, so I'm not sure how to compose stories that way. Just talking, the way I would around the campfire? A delightful notion!"

I sit down and roll the paper forward. Okay, the paper thing is odd and the keyboard feels heavy and lumpy, but the position of the letters is the same, way better than dealing with a French keyboard at a Paris Internet cafe. Whatever I do has got to be better than poking with two fingers.

"Just try talking for a while and I'll type what you say. We can warm up that way."

"Talk about anything?" It's hard to imagine Clemens at a loss for words, but he seems stumped by the strangeness of the situation.

"How about the uniform and mustache story?" My fingers rest lightly on the keys, ready to follow whatever he says next. Can I type fast enough? Considering how slowly Clemens talks, I'm betting yes.

"We could start with the fruit cart story. Ahem." Clemens clears his throat and starts speaking as if he's in front of a big audience. "The police report a fall of fruit. This is not a crime, but rather a pleasant announcement. The fall of fruit led Newton to the great demonstration and discovery of the law of gravitation, a very grave work. If the recent fall of fruit will cause fifty per cent less gravitation of cash from the eater's hand to the seller's pocket, the effect will be more beneficial to the poor than any law of gravity or gravity of the law."

The keys are much heavier than I'm used to, but I keep up pretty well, though this isn't the story I expected Clemens to tell. There are some mistakes because there's no delete key. How do they deal with that?

I'm about to ask, when a tall man with a face like a slab of bacon strides in. I can't tell if he's angry or if that's just the way he always looks.

This time Clemens introduces us. The man is George Eustace Barnes, the boss. Clemens calls me the "promising young assistant reporter new to the city. She's full of surprising talents, this young lady. Like just now – she's using all her fingers on that typewriter, playing it like the piano. I've never seen such a wonder!"

Mr. Barnes takes my hand in his meaty paw, churning it up and down. "Well, girly, we'll see what you can do. It's gotta be better than our friend here. Sam has what I'd call a peculiar genius, but he's not truly suited to being a local reporter. He lets his imagination get in the way of the facts."

"Yet somehow I manage to fill your paper with delightful

stories about everything from the Mechanics Fair to the earthquake we didn't have when one was long overdue. That was an especially exciting week."

"You spill ink, I'll give you that, but we need more local interest stuff. Full of facts! I keep telling you that!"

"Which is why my assistant and I are scheduled early tomorrow morning for a jaunt to the Cliff House. You'll have a description of one of the jewels of the city, a perfect advertisement of why everyone should rush to San Francisco and enjoy its many charms."

"That's what I'm talking about. No more of those wild fantasies of yours about a mysterious petrified man found in someone's cellar. And definitely no calling the Board of Brokers a den of thieves!"

Mr. Barnes grabs a stack of papers and storms back out the door. He was here all of two minutes, but I feel shoved in the chest. Can you bully someone in a sentence or two?

"I can see why you're not keen on his style of writing," I say.

"Style would presume that there's a flavor to it. Sadly, it's stripped of style more than anything else. Bare-bones writing, no salt or pepper to it." Clemens sighs long and loud, a world of drama in one plaintive note. "If only the miserable work didn't pay so well. But it does. And I do love to write. Or I should say, I love to tell stories. Laying out the 'facts,' as Mr. Barnes calls them, is something else entirely. I've always said there's no reason to let truth interfere with a good story."

"Are we really going to the Cliff House?" It's a place I've been to in my own time, a restaurant that's built on the cliffs (hence the name) on the western edge of the city overlooking the Pacific Ocean. I had no idea it's been around so long.

"I suppose we have to now. He's been wanting me to write about that place for a while and I've resisted, oh how I've resisted, since it's so far out there, at the very edges of civilization. Furthermore and much more seriously, he insists I – that is, we – go early. Now I have tried getting up early and I have tried getting up late, and I far prefer the warmth of my bed to the bracing cold air of dawn. But tomorrow we shall leave at 4 a.m. and give Mr. Barnes exactly what he wants."

"But won't I be up late reporting on the theater?"

"Why so you shall. Tonight, you'll visit all of them, write down a stream of facts to satisfy Mr. Barnes, and then prepare for our early morning excursion."

I sigh, resigning myself to getting up much earlier than I'm used to. "Don't I need tickets?"

"You just say you're reporting for the *Call*. If they doubt you, tell them Samuel Clemens sent you because he's busy with a major story, one that will leap right off the front page of the morning paper."

Scout's been listening quietly all this time, but now he interrupts. "What are you thinking, Sam, sending her off that way? She shouldn't go to the theater by herself!"

"I'm thinking that Miss Lodge looks like a sensible girl who can conduct herself safely. You've seen yourself what a marvel she is with a typewriter! Who knows what other secret abilities she has? Besides, I already told her she can describe the Barbary Coast revue without actually attending. That's the only place truly improper for a young lady."

"Well, if you won't go with her, I will! I can't set the type until you've both submitted your stories anyway, so I may as well make sure she's escorted, as a proper young lady should be!"

So that's how I end up on a date with Scout. I mean, I know it's not a date date, but we're going to see shows — at night — so it feels like something.

Except when we get to the first theater, he tells me he'll wait outside, he's too scruffy to go in. I don't look any better and my palms are slick with sweat, but I'm here to do a job. So I go up to the ticket booth nervously and explain I'm there to review for the *Call*. The man at the desk has one of those silly villain mustaches that curl around at the tips, like commas around his nose.

"Since when are there girl reporters? This is what happens when all the men are at the mines, I tell you." He shakes his head sadly. "Don't know what the world is coming to."

Now I'm not nervous – I'm furious. I

curl my fingers into tight fists to keep myself from snapping at him. "Mr. Clemens is busy with a big story, so he sent me to cover for him. He said you'd understand." You stupid mustache-brain, I add in my head.

For a second, I think he won't let me in, but he yawns and shoves a program at me.

"Make sure you spell everyone's name right, not like last time!"

I walk in, feeling like I've just won an important battle for girl reporters everywhere. Nobody notices me standing at the back while people shuffle into their seats. The audience looks richer than the people I've passed on the streets. And I realize there are more women here than I've seen walking around. I scan faces to see if Mom is there, but nobody looks familiar in the sea of strange faces and stranger hairstyles.

Just like in the movies, the lights are turned down around the seats, but turned up around the stage, a signal for people to be quiet. Then the curtain opens and a man bounds on stage, yelling loudly and dramatically. The acting is so hokey, it's hard to watch. The story is about some woman who has lost her boyfriend and he's lost her, too. They each stand on opposite sides of the stage, moaning and groaning in the most ridiculous

way. All they have to do is look at each other and the problem is solved! I last about ten minutes, then duck out to head to the next theater.

"That was quick!" Scout says when he sees me.

"Not quick enough," I say.

"Maybe the next show will be better."

Or maybe I'll stay even less time. The best part of the night might be this, talking with Scout. I study his profile as we walk. I could swear he looks just like Clark, the boy from London.

At Maguire's Opera House, the ticket taker lets me in without any questions. Maybe I look more confident now. Or maybe it's a nicer theater. The audience is definitely fancier. The women wear jeweled tiaras and feathers and long gloves. Mom could be here and I'd never recognize her in that kind of get-up. The men's suits look like the shiny black ones I saw in Paris. The play is called *The Crown Diamonds,* but is just as silly as the first one I saw, though the

sets and costumes look nicer. I wonder if I'm allowed to write about that. Just in case, I make a quick sketch to remind myself.

Back on the street, I gulp down the cool air, much fresher than the smoky stuffiness of the theater. I look up at the stars glittering overhead. So many of them! You never see stars like this in

San Francisco now. You'd have to go far out into the country where it gets really dark. Yet here they are, sparkling magically overhead, as if sprinkling the city with fairy dust.

Scout is leaning against the wall, dozing off, and I nudge him awake.

"I'm sorry to keep you out so late, especially when you have work to do."

"I don't mind." Scout smiles.

The moment seems right, so I ask him, "Where did you come from? What was your life like before you got to San Francisco?" I wonder if he'll say he's from another country, England or France or Italy. But he doesn't speak with an accent. There must be another way he's connected to those other boys.

"I've been here a long time, since I was a kid. I don't remember much of where I'm from, just the stories my folks tell me." Scout looks at me. "Some small town in Ohio, nothing interesting about it."

I want to believe him, but he sounds evasive. I realize with a start that he sounds the way I do when I'm lying to people!

"Do you have any brothers?" I press.

"Only brothers, not sisters?" Scout grins as if it's a silly question.

"I'll give you the full run-down on my family after your next show." He gestures at the American Theater, right in front of us. He'll have plenty of time to come up with a story now, so how can I trust what he tells me?

I try to pay attention to the song-and-dance show, not think about Scout. One man plays the spoons on his leg while another one strums a banjo. They're actually pretty good and the song is catchy. The audience seems to like it, so I put a star on the play-bill, a reminder to say something nice about the performance. This audience isn't as dressed up. Some of the men are even wear-

ing overalls or the same kind of loose pants Scout has on. There aren't many women, so it's easier to search for Mom's curly hair, her slender build. But no luck here, either.

And no luck with Scout who tells me about his three brothers and two sisters, none of whom live in San Francisco. The number three grabs me at first, as I imagine Clark, Giovanni, and Claude as his brothers, spread across the centuries and the world.

But Scout says his brothers are much older, married, with families of their own. And they all live on the East Coast. Seems odd that the whole family would come to California and the only one to stay is Scout. But I shove aside my suspicions. What proof do I have of anything?

The last theater on the list is the New Idea, but I would call it the Bad Idea, since the play is a ridiculous soap opera with a lot of exaggerated sighs, hand wringing, and eye rolling. Nobody in real life acts this way, but the audience eats it up. Mom would have no patience for any of this. When the lead actress pleads with the villain to spare the life of her child, some people actually sniffle and dab at their eyes with handkerchiefs. Ugh! I've had enough.

I thought reviewing would be fun, a chance to see free shows, to look for Mom. But I didn't enjoy any of them. Well, maybe the banjo and spoon playing. That was definitely the best. But I can't write up my own opinions because I'm seeing all this with modern eyes. Instead, I judge by the audience's reaction. If a lot of people nodded off in the back row, that means a bad review. If they looked thrilled, then I can say the performance was spectacular. I jot down a lot of empty adjectives that don't say anything definite, so there's no way to know I haven't seen the whole of any one performance. I start a list in my notebook:

thrilling
dramatic
exciting
inspiring
splendid
uplifting

And for the ones that don't seem so good:

uninspiring
flat
dry
tedious
heavy
clumsy

Along with the sketches of clothes, jewelry, and sets, I have plenty to write about. But I'm still no closer to figuring out the mystery of Scout. As much as I want to trust him, I can't get rid of the niggling worry that something's not right.

Back at the *Call* offices, Gillis is alone, laboring over the press, putting in the metal letters that will spell out Mr. Clemens' stories.

Scout rushes to the trays of type, eager to make up for the time he spent with me. It's like he can't wait to get rid of me! I know I shouldn't take it personally, but it's hard not to.

His fingers fly so fast, they almost move in a cartoon blur. I have my own work to do and pull up a chair to the desk. I see from the stacked sheets next to the typewriter that Clemens has finished all his stories. On the very top is the test page I typed for him.

I get started on my first review. I stumble through the first sentence or two, but when I make a mistake, I just keep going, figuring out that the typesetter (Steve or Scout, either one) will know what I mean. It's strange not having a screen to look at, just one or two lines at a time as the paper flops over the roll. What a ridiculous way to write!

Once I get used to the typewriter, I figure out a formula for my reviews. I start with a few sentences about the audience (glittering, bubbling, appreciative or cat-calling), a few about the actors, singers, and dancers (using my lists) and then a few about the spectacle as a whole (again from the lists).

I write up all the reviews as quickly as I can, my eyes heavy with exhaustion. No wonder Clemens hates this shift! Writing is hard work, even when I'm not trying to do it well, just hack it out.

Finally it's done, my first story is filed. A little flash of excitement flickers through my sleepy fog. My words will be in print! Strangers will read them! I'll savor the feeling tomorrow. Right now, I need to go to bed.

Scout finishes setting his page, too, just in time, and wipes his smudged fingers on his apron before taking it off. "I'll walk Miss Lodge home," he says.

Steve nods. "I'll finish. There's only her reviews left to do anyway."

We step out into the cool summer night together. It smells just the same as back home, comfortingly familiar in all this strangeness. The streets are mostly empty until we get to what Clemens called the Barbary Coast, where all the bars and saloons are, along with the revue I skipped. The lights are still on and men spill out of doors, shoving each other and hurling slurred insults. One beefy man kicks at a slender shadow on the ground. It sounds like he's hitting a sack of sand, but as we come closer, I realize the shadow is another man. He whimpers, but is too drunk or hurt to defend himself.

I shudder and Scout pulls me closer to him, hugging the walls of the buildings. He steers us to a side street, away from the fighting and drinking. The city has a veneer of civilized polish, but underneath, it's rough. And scary. I'm glad I'm not alone.

"So what's your story, besides that your looking for your mother? How did she go missing anyway?" Scout asks.

That's a much bigger question than he realizes! I stick with the version I told Clemens, that my father and brother work in the mines. My mother came to San Francisco to find us a place, but she hasn't written us, so we got worried and my dad sent me to track her down. Which is true in its own way.

"Why don't you look for her at the Post Office? She must go there to pick up the letters you send her. You could leave a notice for her on the board there."

How do I admit that Mom doesn't want to be found? The answer just pops into my head and out it comes.

"The truth is, she ran away. She hated the mining life and she left us. Pa sent me to try to talk her into coming back. But I have no idea how to find her and she won't answer a message. I have to catch her. In person."

There's a long awkward silence. Does he believe me?

"I'm sorry. That's a bit trickier then, isn't it? We could start with the courts, make sure your ma hasn't gotten into any trouble. Sam will know, since he covers that beat. Then we ask around, quiet like, and see what we dig up. Leave it to Sam, Steve, and me. We'll track her down."

"It's nice of you to offer," I say. He's been so kind, so generous. Which just makes me like him even more. I wish he'd hold my hand. He's close enough I almost brush against him as we walk. But he can't really be my friend. I know that. Or part of me does. The part of me that's sweating and nervous definitely doesn't.

There are so few people out now, the figure across the street stands out, snapping my attention away from Scout. It's a woman and for a second, I think it must be Mom. My heart races even faster and I speed up, hoping to catch her. Then the woman walks under the light from a nearby window. It's the Watcher. Her boarding house isn't near here, so what's she doing? Does she know where Mom is?

"I know that woman!" I gasp to Scout as I run across the

street. This time, I'll make her answer my questions.

But instead of facing me down, scaring me with her threats about Mom, the Watcher looks at me in a panic. She slips into the shadows of an alleyway and when I follow her, there's nothing. Just crates and barrels and a snoring drunk.

"Who is she? If she knows you, why didn't she greet you?" Scout asks, catching up to me.

"I don't know. She's a friend of my mother. Maybe she doesn't want to tell me where she is." I wipe the sticky sweat from my face, trying to look calm. The Watcher wasn't looking for me or she wouldn't have run away. So Mom has to be around here. But where?

My chest feels heavy and tight. "I have to find my mother, at least talk to her. Maybe I can't convince her to go home, but I have to try. I've come all this way."

And this part really is true.

July 2, 1864

I collapse onto my narrow bed. There's a mix of jasmine, hot oil, chicken, and something indefinable, swept into my room along with the sounds of sloshing water, objects thudding, and doors creaking. But I'm so tired, none of it keeps me from falling asleep – for what feels like five minutes before a pounding on my door wakes me up. Oh right, the early morning trip to the Cliff House. I'd forgotten all about it. But then, I don't have an alarm to set anyway.

I splash some water from the basin on my face and get dressed in the only clothes I have. At least here wearing the same thing for weeks on end seems normal.

"Rise and shine!" Clemens greets me when I open the door. He looks chipper for such an early hour. "I've rented us a nice little horse and buggy, so bring your notebook and let's be off."

The sun isn't up yet, and I wonder what we'll be able to see in the darkness. I shiver as I settle into the open carriage, my shawl thin in the thick morning fog.

"No coat?" Clemens arches an eyebrow, then digs in the back of the carriage and unfolds a heavy horse blanket over my shoulders. It's warmer, yes, but also smells strongly of the stable. So much for fresh morning air!

"Now that's better, isn't it?" He gets in and slaps the reins on the horse's rump and away we trundle along the empty, quiet streets. "See, there are no other wagons to block the way, no carriages we need to swerve around. We have the town to ourselves. And just smell the sweetness of the flowers, opening up to the dewy dawn!"

All I smell is horse. And it's nowhere near dawn. I pull the blanket tighter despite the stink. A frigid wind whips in from the ocean. Cold tendrils of fog sweep around us, numbing my toes. "Maybe we should try this again in the afternoon, when it's warmer."

"Mr. Barnes insists on a morning visit! I don't give him much that he likes, so this is the least I can do, though right now, in this freezing cold, it feels more like the most I could do. Now back in Hannibal, Missouri, where I was a boy, it would be pleasant to be out on a July morning. Blissfully cool before the blistering, humid heat of the day set in. San Francisco, however, doesn't truly have a summer, not one that we normal citizens would recognize as such. In fact, the coldest winter I ever spent was a summer in San Francisco."

A chill goes through me, and it's not from the fog. "What did you say?" Everyone in the Bay Area knows that line about San Francisco summers. It's a famous Mark Twain line, or rather a famous line that Mark Twain supposedly said, but really didn't. Except, I just heard him say it. Now I remember where I'd heard the name Sam Clemens!

"You're Mark Twain!" I gasp.

"You read that story?" Clemens looks surprised. "In the *Territorial Enterprise?* That was just a line or two. I'm surprised you would remember it or the fellow who wrote it, as memorable as I'd like my words to be."

"It's your pen name, right? The one you use for stories."

"Well, I've used it once. I don't sign the brilliant pearls I write for the *Call*. But maybe one day, I'll use it again. It has a nice ring to it, doesn't it? Much more forceful, intelligent, inspired than Sam Clemens. I'm thinking I'll save it for when I write something that truly reflects what I want to say, a story I've chosen freely, not had assigned to me through the dreary duty of being a reporter."

I'm so excited, I don't feel the cold anymore, though the fog is thicker than ever, so thick I can barely see the horse's ears ahead of us. All the pictures I've seen of Mark Twain show him as an old man, with thick white hair and a mustache to match. But this is a young Mark Twain, with a boyish face and red hair. He looks more like a leprechaun than a distinguished writer. I feel like I should ask a million questions. And if my brain weren't as frozen as the rest of me, I might be able to.

The sky is lighter, hinting at day, by the time we get to the Outer Lands where the Cliff House is. We tumble out of the carriage awkwardly, our joints stiff with cold. There's a big camera obscura next to the restaurant, a room with lenses that project the view outside onto the walls of the room, slowly rotating so the whole panorama unfurls in front of you. When I was last here with Dad, the whole thing looked sad and worn. Now it's freshly painted, cheerfully new in the thin morning light.

I duck inside but all I see is fog projected onto the walls. Of course.

I walk out to the edge of the bluff, where Clemens stands shivering. I can see seals barking on the rocks below, but not much beyond them. We're two human icicles, and our one thought is to find a warm fire inside.

We don't.

The restaurant is only slightly warmer inside than out. There's no fog or wind, which is a relief, but no heat, either. The bartender brings out hot strong coffee which normally I'd spit out as too bitter, but I hold the cup with both numb hands, trying desperately to warm myself. The small sips slowly thaw out my jaw, throat, and chest. If only I could dip my feet in coffee water!

Clemens is quiet, unusual for him, probably because his voice has frozen.

"Why is this place even open this early?" I say, breaking the silence. "Who would come?"

"You know the old saying of Benjamin Franklin – 'Early to bed, early to rise, makes a man healthy, wealthy, and wise.' This little jaunt was meant to offer proof of the adage, according to my assignment. That or the man wanted to punish me. Right now, my toes vote for the latter. An ingenious torture, too, that he's chosen!

One cloaked with the semblance of virtue, of improving my soul, while in reality injuring my body."

"You could get up early, without venturing so far out! We could have stayed home and had a hot breakfast. That would have been much healthier!"

"Even healthier still would have been another hour or two of sleep," Clemens grumbles.

After two cups of coffee, the sun has lifted above the horizon, and the fog is wispy rather than thick. I almost feel human again when we get back into the carriage. I don't know what kind of newspaper story Clemens will make of all this. Could his job as a reporter or the books he'll write later matter to Mom? Maybe if I ask the right questions, I'll figure it out.

As we drive back to the city and the day warms up, I pepper Clemens with questions. Why did he come out West in the first place? Why San Francisco? How long does he plan to stay? What does he want to do with his life? What kind of reporting does he really want to do? What I'm really wondering, though, is if he's a time traveler, too. After all, Arthur Conan Doyle was, though their personalities couldn't be more different.

"Now hold on there, missy! Who is the reporter here? I never did get my girl on the street interview with you and here you are, getting your man in the buggy interview. Or trying to. Let me give you a professional tip – wait for an answer before plunging on to the next question. You'll get more information that way."

"I'm sorry, I'm just so excited." I stop myself before I say something truly stupid, like has he ever thought about time travel and when would he go to if the could. Instead, I ask a normal question. "You said you're from Missouri. So why come out West? It can't have been an easy trip."

"Exactly the question I wanted to pose to you. But since I'm managing the reins and you have free hands to take notes, I may as well satisfy your curiosity. I originally came out to Washoe with my brother, Orion. He'd been appointed by President Lincoln to the lucrative position of Secretary of the Territory of Nevada, the first the territory ever had. I'd worked for Orion before, when he ran the Ben Franklin Books and Job Printing office, and we didn't always see eye to eye, but this seemed like such a high falutin' position, I was sure some of the glory would rain down on me. Or at the least, I'd have the adventure of being out West, where the possibilities seemed endless. Better than piloting a steamboat on the Mississippi River, at any rate."

"But you left, so I'm guessing there wasn't much glory after all." I scribble notes furiously. Some of this has to matter, time traveler or not. Abraham Lincoln! An important political position! Was Mom trying to stop Lincoln from being assassinated? Or had that already happened? Where's Malcolm when I need him?

"I tried my hand at mining, but while fortunes were made all around me, I didn't have much luck. And the only thing worse than being poor, is being poor while everyone around you becomes instant millionaires! It's hard not to take one's misery as a judgement on one's character at such times, rather than mere bad luck. I was better at writing for the newspaper there. I didn't get rich quick, but the pay was good."

"So why did you leave?"

"Let's just say it seemed safer to get away for a bit. And after the dusty emptiness of Washoe, San Francisco is a feast for eyes, ears, and stomach! So if I have to bore myself to tears with note-taking and fact-collecting, if I have to brave the freezing fog of a San Francisco summer morning, it's a small price to pay."

I want to know what the trouble was, but Clemens says it's not worth talking about. Meaning, I'm guessing, it's too ordinary, not something he can turn into a funny story. Anyway, what really matters is whether he's a time traveler. I've got to think of a way to ask that doesn't make me look suspicious. Or crazy.

Houses, stores, rows of buildings loom ahead and Clemens slaps the reins on the horse's back, urging her to speed up, to get us home. The houses are closer together now, though there are still big expanses of fields and garden plots. We're going faster than I thought a buggy could go, the wind whipping in my face. I'm thrown to one side, then the other. Why haven't seat belts been invented? We round a corner at a park near the old Mission (not so old now), taking it so quickly, the buggy tips wildly, spilling us onto the ground.

One second I'm taking notes. The next I'm thrown onto the

grass. It happens so fast, there's no time to brace myself. The sky spins crazily around me and I land on the blanket, my knees and elbows hitting hardest. I sit up dizzily, trying to understand exactly what happened. I steady my breathing, feeling my arms and legs. Nothing's broken. I'm scraped, but not bleeding. Clemens is sitting a few feet from me, grass in his hair and mud on his pants, but otherwise fine. The horse happily chomps on the grass, not fazed at all by the accident.

I get up on wobbly legs. "Are you okay?" I ask.

"Nothing broken but my pride." Clemens dusts grass off of his pants and jacket. "That fool horse should know better! I'm of a mind to have her arrested for presenting a public hazard or for battery, as I'm feeling mighty battered!"

I don't say anything about him being the driver. It's funny, I'd never thought about carriages having accidents. That seems like something that started with the invention of cars, but obviously not.

I help Clemens right the buggy, while the horse stares at us, clear in her mind who the responsible party is.

"Shall we be off then?" Clemens settles his hat back firmly on his head.

I gather up the blanket, but where's my notebook? It must

have been thrown from the carriage, along with my pen. I look around us and realize that we aren't in a park, like the one near the Mission in my present, but in a cemetery. In fact, as I come closer to a tombstone, I see it's a Jewish cemetery.

"I didn't know there were Jews in San Francisco so early!" I scan the names – there are Levis, Goldbergs, Brandensteins. No Goldins, but I don't expect there to be. Dad's family didn't come from Russia until the end of the century. And Mom's was in Lithuania until the 1930s.

"I can recall clearly the first Jews I ever saw." Clemens rubs his forehead, as if conjuring up the strange image. "One family somehow landed in Hannibal. How, I can't imagine! Missouri of all places had to be the furthest from their homeland, completely foreign to them, as they were foreign to us. We thought of Jews as creatures of myth, long ago vanished, like fairies or centaurs, and to see them in flesh and blood caused quite a stir. Some people shuddered in horror, as if blasphemy rose from their skin, and wondered whether we should crucify them. I remember there were two boys in the family and one of the sons was named Levin. We called him Twenty-two because twice 'leven makes twenty-two." Clemens chuckles at the memory. "And now, here in San Francisco, Jews walk down the street, go to City Hall meetings, work in some of the finest banks, and nobody wonders at them. We're a long way from Hannibal, we are. Out on the edges of civilization, out West, where different rules apply. Now that's why I love it here!"

I'm not sure whether I should admit to being Jewish. I don't want to be some strange exotic creature with a whiff of incense about her. But does Mom want to change something about the Jews living here? It sounds like they're part of regular society, not living in ghettos the way they did in 17th century Rome. I'm pretty sure some of the most important founders of San Francisco's cultural life were Jews, though I thought that happened later. Anyway, I can't remember who exactly. Yet another thing I'll have to ask Malcolm about.

Actually, the graves might tell me the answer to that and I scan names as I look for my pen and notebook. I find my pen next to a marker for Stern – that's the family Stern Grove is named for! And my notebook is nestled under Hirsch Strauss' stone. He must be from the Levi Strauss family, the one that made a fortune inventing blue jeans.

What happened to all these graves? Something else to ask Malcolm. I jot down the names from the tombstones so I can look them up once I'm back in my own time. Before I turn to go, I place a pebble on Strauss' marker, adding mine to the others that are already there, part of the chain of Jews showing respect for the dead.

I pocket my pen and notebook, feeling like a small gift has been given to me, a sense of connection to the Jewish past of San Francisco.

Back in the buggy, I take out my notebook and go back to my questions.

"What kind of stories do you most want to write, if you didn't have to listen to your editor?" If he says science fiction, is that a time-traveling hint?

"The kind of stories I like to read. There's a fellow from the office next to us at the *Call*. He works at the U.S. Mint, but he's really a writer. Only, of course, his chicken scratches don't pay the rent. Still, he sets down tales of life in the mining towns of the Sierras and tells it just the way it is, with the same color and humor that I've seen there."

I can't help feeling disappointed. Realism is the opposite of science fiction. But then, the science-fiction writer H.G. Wells didn't turn out to be the time traveler, instead it was the logical Arthur Conan Doyle. There's no way to know if Clemens is a fellow traveler unless I flat out ask him. I clear my throat nervously. But I can't do it. Instead I ask for the name of the writer he admires.

"Bret Harte. He's one of the pleasantest men I have ever known. And also one of the unpleasantest men I have ever known. He's the sort of man where the clothes wear him instead of the other way 'round. For me, that would be uppity on the part of my shirts and trousers. I don't want my jacket to be smarter than I am! Bret is one of those men who care more about how they appear than how they actually are. Which means being friends with him is fine if you like associating with a bright blue tie or a fancy pair of shoes. If you prefer real conversation or even simply a game of cards, then it's time to find other friends, plainer sorts with stouter hearts, like Steve, the typesetter whom you met. Now he's the sort I'd trust my life with. Come to think of it, I have."

By now, the streets are more crowded and we jostle between carts as we head back to the stable where Clemens rented the horse and buggy. I wonder if the owner will check for dents, the way rent-a-car companies do. Will he be able to tell we tipped over? Clemens doesn't seem worried about it. And sure enough, the horse is handed over with a nod and nothing more.

The sun is higher, the day warmer, but without the heavy horse blanket around my shoulders, I shiver. I smell like stable and sweat. I want to go home, scrub my face at least, but Clemens walks us straight to the *Call* office.

"Don't you want to see your story in print? It's an exciting moment, the first time you read your own words in a newspaper, there for all to see! I'd say it's intoxicating even. When I held my very first feature in the *Territorial Enterprise,* I felt ten feet tall, and for a man of my limited stature, that's saying a lot!"

I'd forgotten about my theater reviews. Remembering them,

I'm not particularly proud. When I wrote them, I was more focused on getting the piece in on time and going home to bed. Still, this is the first time I've ever had anything published, and a quiver of excitement goes through me as we walk into the office and I see the pile of newspapers.

Scout's there, too. He smiles at me and holds out the newest issue of the *Morning Call.* "How does it feel to be read by our ten thousand subscribers?" he asks.

Ten thousand? I didn't know that many people lived in 1860s San Francisco! I take the thin newspaper and open it up. It's only a single page, folded in half, and the printed price is all of twelve and a half cents a week. How do people pay a half cent? It makes the price seem like a joke. I scan through the columns quickly. And there it is, on the back page, my three solid columns about the theatre.

I can't help grinning as I show the article to Clemens. "Is this what you wanted?"

The reporter bends over the page thoughtfully. "Why, yes! You've captured the essence of the theater-going experience. You set the stage, introduce the actors, describe the audience, and then you have your wide-ranging assortment of adjectives to rate the performances. I would have added a few of my favorites, like 'sumptuous,' 'glittering,' and 'bumptuous.' Aren't those wonderful words? You feel like you can roll them around on your tongue, taste their juiciness.

But you've managed just fine without them. Most satisfying of all, you filled three columns, an impressively inky achievement!"

"Can I keep a copy?" Even as I ask, I remember the time-traveling rule of No Taking Anything Back to Your Present. I'm not allowed to take even this thin sheet of newsprint. And if I try, it would probably disintegrate into dust during the journey. Anyway, it's really for the best. I can't leave a permanent sign that I've been here. Luckily, none of the articles are signed, so there's no way of knowing who wrote what. This edition of the *Call* doesn't prove I've been here. It's just a regular newspaper, full of ordinary events.

Still, I take a paper and fold it into my pocket. Not to take home, but to savor, at least while I'm here.

Clemens rushes off to the police department, starting his usual rounds of sniffing for news, leaving me to write up the Cliff House story. But what is there to say? It was cold, the view was fogged in, but at least the coffee was hot. Better to go in the afternoon when there will be a view and the cold won't seep into your bones.

Scout reads my first few sentences and laughs. "Sounds like a charming outing! Did you at least get some cake to go with the coffee?"

"No," I say, as my stomach grumbles its own answer.

"Then how about some toast?" Scout carves a slice of bread from a loaf on the desk and sets it on top of the Franklin stove. In seconds, the room is filled with the lovely small of warm bread. Now I'm really hungry!

"Thanks!" I pick up the bread and take a big bite. It's sourdough! A reminder of how long that's been the signature bread of the city. I want to laugh – it's wonderful seeing how much of San Francisco's character is already here, from the wide range of food to sourdough bread to foggy summer days.

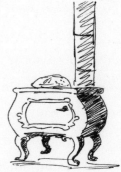

The rest of the morning passes quickly with me struggling to make a story out of nothing. At noon, I look at Scout, hoping he'll suggest another nickel lunch. He does and we head to a different saloon, one that's even cheaper. Two cents for a cup of coffee will get you plenty to eat. This place doesn't have fancy art on the walls, just wallpaper printed with flowers. The shelves are decorated with crockery and it feels more like a cafe than a gallery. Maybe that's

why it costs less.

I've heaped my plate high with stew, corn bread, and pickles and settled down next to Scout when I notice a familiar figure holding her own plate in front of the oysters.

It's Mom.

She's wearing a green plaid dress that I don't recognize, but her hair is pinned up the way it was in London and Paris, and when she turns to show her profile, there's no question at all.

I hold very still, keeping my face down over my plate. If she sees me, she'll run. I have to figure out a way to talk to her without chasing her away.

"What's the matter?" Scout asks. "You're acting strange."

"It's that woman," I whisper. "The one in the green plaid. She's my mother."

"So talk to her! What are you waiting for?"

"I told you, she ran away. I don't want to scare her off. Why don't you try talking to her? Find out where she's staying, what she's doing here. You can play the same game as Clemens, say you're doing a 'woman on the streeet' interview, collecting people's stories of why they came to San Francisco."

I have to give Scout credit. He doesn't balk or question me, just puts down his fork and walks up to Mom. I can't hear what he says to her, but she doesn't look happy to see him. In fact she eyes him up and down suspiciously.

"Do I know you?" she demands loudly.

"I don't think so," Scout says, standing in front of me so he's blocking Mom's view of me, but also my view of her. "But I'm happy to make your acquaintance."

"You look familiar," Mom says, like that's a bad thing. Then she gasps so loudly I can hear it from my seat several feet away. She sets down her plate and starts backing away. She recognizes Scout? Maybe the same way I do, but I thought it was good that he reminded me of friends from my other time-travel adventures, like there was something connecting them all.

Scout takes a step toward Mom and for a minute I think she's going to haul off and hit him, she looks that furious. Instead she turns and rushes out the door. Exactly what I didn't want to happen.

There's only one thing to do – run after her.

There she is, on Montgomery Street. Not running, but walking at a fast clip. Should I follow her, see where she's going, figure out what she wants to change, or just stop her?

I hear Malcolm's voice in my head, "Stop her! Whatever she wants to change, it's wrong."

I break into a run. Before she can turn around and see that it's me, I grab her arm.

"Mom! Come home with me! We need to talk!"

She whips around. "We can't be together! You know that!"

"Then listen to me! Please!"

"Mira," her voice is low, desperate. "You don't understand. The reason we can change the future is because we're both time travelers. We can do it by being in the same place at the same time, but we can't actually be together. Not unless it's absolutely essential. We're not that desperate. Yet."

She's actually talking to me! That's a huge relief and a big change right there.

I shake my head. "I don't want to save myself this way, not when I could be hurting a lot of other people. You don't know what your changes will do in the future. Not for sure. You have to trust me to take care of myself. This is about my future, so let me handle it! I'm the only one who can change my future – me, in my own time!"

"You're still my child – I'll take care of you!"

"I'm not a baby anymore! Just tell me where it happens. Then I can avoid that place. So we'll both be happy – your information will save me and there will be no more messing with the past."

"If telling you would make a difference, don't you think I would? You don't understand. What if Malcolm could get hurt too? Would you help me for his sake?"

That's a cheap shot. Malcolm would be the first to say history shouldn't be changed, no matter what!

"Mira, you have to trust me. You don't know the whole story."

"Then explain it to me! Why should I trust you when you obviously don't trust me!" I try not to yell, but I'm furious now.

"It's not that I don't trust you. You're too young for this kind of responsibility." Mom keeps her voice level, maddeningly calm.

"But I'm not too young to help you change things? You can't have it both ways, Mom! You push me to do things, but you won't tell me how or why. Give me some credit!"

"I'm trying to teach you how to be responsible and yes, independent. But you're not ready yet."

The more mad I get, the more steely cold Mom is, which just makes me angrier. It's so infuriating when grown-ups tell you how much you don't know when they're the ones withholding the information. But she's not running away, she's here talking to me, so I match my tone to hers.

"And what is it you want me to change here anyway? You've given me hints before. If you really want me to do something, you have to say what it is."

Mom's mouth tightens. She steps back from me and I expect her to bolt. But she stands there one more minute. Long enough to say, "I wish I could tell you more, but I can't. This is our last chance. We have to get it right this time."

"Tell me!" I want to scream, stamp my feet like a toddler having a tantrum.

"You'll do the right thing." Mom leans in, as close as she dares. "And then we'll go home, the two of us together. I promise." She nods brusquely, dismissing me, then walks down the street, turns a corner and disappears. And this time I don't run after her.

I can't help it -- big, ugly sobs force their way up my throat and I'm crying in the street like my heart is broken. What am I supposed to do? What am I supposed to believe? And why didn't I ask her about Scout? Another chance, wasted!

I cry like that until my eyes feel itchy and dry. Then I wipe my wet face on my sleeve and go back into the restaurant. I try to look normal, except I'm not sure what that should look like.

"What happened?" Scout asks, pulling out a stool for me.

"I'm not sure." I pick up a piece of corn bread and start shredding it nervously. "She seemed to know you. Does she?"

"No, no, of course not," Scout says in a way that sounds like a lie. Who is he really? Why does he look like Clark and Claude and Giovanni? There's an important connection I'm missing. I wish I knew what!

Whatever it is, I'm suddenly wary again. I want Scout to be a friend, but really there's nobody I can trust here. Not even Clemens. Any of them could be fellow time-travelers. Or Watchers.

The rest of lunch is awkward. I don't know how to talk to Scout any more. All I want is to go back to my present and talk to Malcolm. I need him to help me figure all this out. I've got to find a Touchstone.

I walk up and down Montgomery, but there are no fountains, no sculptures, nothing like the things I've used as Touchstones before. Am I going to be stuck in 1864 San Francisco? Malcolm suggested I try something wooden, but I don't see anything that feels like it's holding time, nothing that pulls me toward it with an eerie glow.

I turn down Bush into Chinatown where it's more crowded. Maybe a well could be a Touchstone? But once again nothing feels right. Somehow, in the midst of all these people, I run into Clemens.

What are the odds I'd find one of the few people I know in this time?

"Ah, Miss Lodge!" He tips his hat. "I read your story about our early morning adventure. You succeeded in setting down the facts of the story,  but it needed more flavor, something to encourage the reader on, all the way into the frozen mists of the Cliff House. So I took the liberty to season the stew, so to speak."

"I was trying to save you work and ended up giving you more." I wonder if I'll still get paid. Maybe he'll even fire me. I'm too embarrassed to look him in the face.

"Not at all! It's much less work to revise something than to start from a blank piece of paper. You saved me hours – well, considering how I write, maybe minutes. But still, that's time saved! Let's go back to the *Call* offices and I'll show you what I've done. Next time, it will be easier for you, I'm sure, as soon as you have caught the rhythm of newspaper work."

He's so kind to me, I allow myself to be steered back to the newspaper office, but I keep an eye peeled for any potential Touchstones on the way.

Scout doesn't look up when we come in, intent on fitting the metal slugs of type into the right slots. I can't tell if he's mad at me or hurt. Or something else entirely. You'd think you could tell something from the way someone bends over, from the set of their mouth, but all I can see is that Scout is ignoring me. So I ignore him back. Not that he notices.

Clemens hands me his typed pages. The story is the same, but completely different. He's made my dreary sentences funny. I can almost hear his slow  drawl as I read and see the wink he gives when he says something especially ridiculous.

"It's so much better! I wish I could write like that!"

"We all have the talents we must bear. I've been cursed with a tongue that runneth over. At least that's what my schoolteachers always said. Why, they wanted to know, did I have to talk so much in class? Because, I told them, there is always something interesting to turn into a story. Or if there isn't, then stretch the dull grain of truth into something amazing, fantastic, spectacular!"

"You've done better than that — you've made the ordinary funny!" I'm impressed, but as I read the story over, I realize he has to revise it yet again. "I'm afraid, though, that I have to ask you to take my name out of it." There's no way I can leave such tangible proof that I've been here, in this time period where I don't belong.

I worry that he'll ask why, but instead Clemens offers right away to give my part in the article to one of his friends. "I'll just change your name to Harry. He has a good name, which he rarely uses, so it's still shiny and new. I'm sure he won't mind you borrowing it for the purposes of a little early morning adventure."

"Thank you! I just don't want the family back east to get the wrong idea."

"Of course! A young lady can never be too careful of her reputation. To be seen in the company of the likes of me is certain to set tongues wagging."

"I didn't mean that!" I blush hotly.

Steve Gillis bustles in, heading straight for the press. I'm grateful to have the whole stupid thing forgotten as the two men talk about plans for the evening and what other stories might yet fill the paper.

"You've given me the court reports, the police news, the Cliff House piece, but that's not enough, even with young missy filing some theater reviews tonight. We need something bigger, something that'll take up more columns." Steve points to the page Scout is setting. "Maybe there's a new mine stock being offered or a politician come to town? See what you can find out."

"Off we go then, to nose out more news. Are you coming, Miss Lodge?"

How can I say no? I want to find Mom, to talk to Malcolm, but I can't resist a little more time with Mark Twain before he becomes Mark Twain. He's as charming as I'd imagined him to be – more, even, because he's young and not yet famous. I wonder if he gets a swelled head once he's a bestseller. Or becomes boring and pompous. I want him to stay just the way he is, a little bit rebellious and a lot funny.

Despite Clemens' constant stream of stories about San Francisco gossip, this part of being a reporter is boring. We walk around, asking people if anything interesting has happened lately. We learn that Mrs. Campbell has had a baby boy, that Mr. Hink is thinking of opening a dry goods store, that the mail was delayed yet another day. Nothing worth putting in a newspaper.

Then something happens – right in front of us. Not a bank robbery or a daring escape from a burning building, but it's a story, alright.

A Chinese man with a long braid down his back crosses the street with one of those pole things across his shoulders. On  either end of the pole hangs a basket full of neatly folded laundry. It's the kind of thing you expect to see in a foreign country, not the streets of San Francisco, but there are lots of things like that in

Chinatown. Still, I take out my notebook and start sketching while Clemens asks the the woman sweeping the sidewalk in front of the tailor shop if she's seen anything of note.

The woman shakes her head as three young white men start yelling at the laundryman from the other side of the street, calling him ugly names. The Chinese man doesn't respond, just quickens his pace, walking away from the insults. So the toughs pick up some stones and throw them at the man. One hits his basket, another thuds against his back.

"Stop that!" I yell, outraged.

One of the men turns to me and laughs. "What, you like-ee those buck-toothed monkeys?"

I want to throw a rock myself, right into his beefy face, but Clemens puts a warning hand on my arm.

"You don't want to stir up those hood-  lums. There's a police officer on the other side of the street. He'll take care of them."

Sure enough, a cop leans against the fruit seller's stand, munching on an apple. He glances at the laundryman, but shows no concern at all. His snack interests him more than anything else.

"Go back home to China!" one of the creeps calls, hurling a heavier rock that narrowly misses the laundryman.

Now the cop looks up – and smiles! He's actually amused by

the attack. The laundryman starts running awkwardly, jostling the heavy weight of the baskets.

I have to do something! I know the time-travel rules, but this is about plain human decency. I head over to the three goons, hands clenched into hard fists. Clemens shakes his head, but he doesn't stop me this time. He's fed up, too, I can feel it. So why doesn't he yell at the cop, scream at the thugs? Maybe that's the nature of being a reporter – like a time-traveler, you just watch.

"Whatcha gonna do, girly?" one of the goons says, sneering at me.

I'm about to tell him exactly what I want to do when a woman comes out of a store right in front of me.

It's the Watcher, her beautiful face marred by un ugly scowl. She looks like she'd like to throw some stones herself. At me.

She takes a step closer. "Are you the one I have to punish, not your mother? You said you understood. Yet here you are. About to interfere."

The words stab me. Because they're true. I'm as bad as Mom, changing things when they suit me, not thinking about what it might mean in the future. Then it hits me – if it's hard for me to see a stranger tormented, it must be much more difficult for Mom to see her own kids in danger. I stand stock still, frozen by the thought. I'm still mad at Mom, but I understand her better now.

I lock eyes with the Watcher. I'm not afraid of her anymore. "You're right," I admit. "I'm glad you stopped me."

Her brow furrows in surprise.

"And maybe you can help me in another way. I want to go, but I can't find a Touchstone."

The Watcher drills me with her eyes, trying to read whether I'm worth helping. "You can't control your mother, so you may as well go. And stay away from now on!" She turns to leave. "If you're smart enough to figure out how!" She opens a parasol and strolls down the street like she owns it. Why did I think she'd tell me anything?

I walk back to Clemens. Please, don't ask me anything, I plead silently. I don't want to have to come up with an explanation for who the Watcher was and what we said. But Clemens isn't looking at me. He's glaring at the bullies. And at the policeman.

The yelled insults continue. More rocks are thrown. The bullies even start to chase the poor laundryman, who finally ducks down a narrow alley, escaping his tormentors. The three toughs sling their arms across each other's shoulders and stroll away down the middle of the street, probably hunting more people to attack. The cop finishes his apple and throws the core onto the ground.

I know I can't do anything, but I blurt out anyway. "What's wrong with that policeman? Why didn't he do anything? They could have really hurt that man!"

Clemens doesn't answer me, but strides over to the cop.

"You are an officer of the peace, are you not?" This isn't his usual soft drawl, but a voice of thundering anger. " Aren't you paid to protect the innocent and prosecute the guilty? How could you let those hoodlums accost an honest citizen of our town?"

The policeman looks up, surprised. His ruddy round cheeks make him look like a hamster with a mustache. "He was just a Chinaman. No harm done."

"No harm done?" Clemens' voice bristles with righteous indignation. "He could have lost an eye, been killed, for all you did! I'm a reporter for the *Morning Call* and all the world will know of your cowardly, ignoble behavior! Your name – give me your name!"

The cop launches a gob of spit right next to Clemens' shoe. "Tom MacGregor. Go ahead and tell the world I won't lift a finger to help no Chinaman. I'll be called a hero and you'll be branded a fool." He leans back against the wall, satisfied.

"Come on, Miss Lodge," Clemens calls to me. "We've got a story to write!" All the way back, he fumes and mutters to himself about the stupidity of the local constabulary (which I take to be a fancy word for policemen), the hard-working, much-reviled Chinese immigrants, and the bad manners of the thick-headed yahoos with straw for brains who populate the city.

This is it, I think, the thing Mom wants me to change. She's always fighting injustice and this treatment of Chinese-Americans is horribly wrong. I bet I'm supposed to encourage Mark Twain to write this story, to be a champion for tolerance, just like Emile Zola and his famous *J'Accuse* headline. Except I can't.

Back at the *Call* offices, I tell myself I won't do anything that will change history. But if Clemens is writing this story anyway, what I say or don't say won't make a difference. So when he asks me, I show him my sketches, remind him of how the bullies looked. After all, I'm not telling him something he doesn't already know.

Clemens starts hammering at the typewriter keys, and this time I don't offer to type for him – that feels too much like interfering. I'm treading a fine line and I know it. In the end my scruples don't matter though, since Clemens, who never does anything fast, writes in a fury of clattering keys, jabbing with his two fingers much quicker than I thought possible.

The finished story is, as Clemens puts it, full of "considerable warmth and holy indignation." He tells me that usually he doesn't bother to read his printed stories. He writes them out of duty, with a dull heart. But this story is different.

"There's fire in this, Miss Lodge, and literature! This is a dividing moment for me, from scribbler of amusing little vignettes to writer, a real writer, the kind Bret Harte is."

Yes, I tell myself, this is it, the moment that counts! I'm watching Mark Twain become Mark Twain. Maybe he'll even sign the story with his famous pen name. Should I suggest that? Is that what Mom wants?

But I'm not changing anything – that's over now. For good.

"What do you think?" Clemens shoves the pages at me. "Do I capture the leaden oafishness of the officer? Do my words stir anger so that readers will call for justice? Will they urge changing the law so that the Chinese can testify when they're abused like this?"

"I didn't know about that law, but I sure hope so!" I quickly scan the story. There's Clemens' trademark humor in how he describes the lumpish policeman, but there's outrage, too.

"You know how I told you I don't sign my stories?" Clemens takes back the pages. I don't say anything, but it's like he read my mind. "This story is different. It matters to me." He goes back to the typewriter. I look over his shoulder as he adds his byline: "Mark Twain."

Yes! It feels right, like this is what's supposed to happen. I'm not messing with history, I'm just part of it.

July 3, 1864

I had planned on searching for a Touchstone, but I ended up back at the theaters, thinking maybe I'd see something on the way. I owed Clemens at least one more night of not having to cover the shows. But I promised myself that first thing in the morning, I'd be back in my own time.

As soon as I find a Touchstone, that is. I wander the docks, the narrow side streets, but I don't see anything with that familiar eerie glow. The Watcher was right, I'm not good at time-travel. Discouraged, I go to the *Call* offices to see how Mark Twain's first San Francisco story turned out.

Clemens is already there when I arrive. He's not excited like I expect. He's furious! Scout and Steve Gillis look just as upset.

"Is something wrong?"

"It's my story, the only one I've ever written that was worth printing! It's gone, cut from the paper, condemned to extinction by Mr. Barnes!" Clemens' usually mild blue eyes flash in anger.

Steve Gillis puts a consoling hand on his friend's arm. "Barnes has a point. This isn't that kind of newspaper. We don't do muckraking, especially when the muck raked up will offend our readers."

"How would hearing about such a serious injustice offend them?" I ask. "They should want to know!"

"My thoughts exactly!" Clemens agrees. "But according to our wise and eminently sensible manager, the *Call* is a washer-woman's paper – that is, it's the paper of the poor. San Francisco, after all, has other newspapers. The *Call* is simply the cheapest. It relies on those poor readers and so we must – again, according to the inestimable Mr. Barnes – respect their prejudices or perish. Most of the poor are Irish immigrants. Their community offers the bulk of the support for the *Morning Call*. Without their devoted following, the newspaper would close in a few weeks."

"Poor people care about injustice," I protest. "All the more reason to print the story."

"Except each group hates another group. So the Irish hate the Chinese who hate the Italians who hate the Germans. We're all reduced to our little clans, even here in the West, where lines are supposed to be looser. Believe me, these groups are much tighter in Missouri, where I'm from. People trust those who are like them and anyone else is a suspicious outsider. The Chinese here, they're the most outside you can get. They dress differently, eat differently, speak differently. But their worst crime is that they take jobs the Irish say they want, even though they won't actually do them. Such as building the transcontinental railroad. " Clemens waves a hand dismissively. "Anyway, the reason for their prejudice doesn't matter. The point is that this article could provoke the whole Irish hive into a stinging rebuke of the newspaper. Meaning, they might not buy it anymore and the paper, such as it is, would fold."

"Could we take the story to one of those other newspapers?" Even as I say it, I realize I should keep my mouth shut. This could be a real change, one I don't dare make.

Luckily Clemens shakes his head. "The only other editor who would take my work is Bret Harte, for the *Alta California,* but that journal features longer articles, more like essays. Not this kind of story. I've fooled myself, thinking I was a real journalist. I'm simply a stooge for the *Call,* scribbling meaningless drivel that people can use to wrap their fish in or sweep up last night's ashes from the grate." Clemens puts on his jacket and hat. "Well, off to start on my daily, dreary rounds, grinding out words into a tasteless mush of inoffensive and easily swallowed pap."

The door slams shut and the three of us stare at each other.

Steve Gillis breaks the silence. "He'll be alright. Sam knows he has to be practical. And at least he tried to do the noble thing. That's more than Barnes can say."

"Do you think he'll give up reporting?" I wonder if that

could be a good thing after all, get Clemens started writing stories instead, the kind he'll be famous for many years later.

Steve shrugs. "Reporting beats mining, I'll tell you that. He's not in a hurry to go back to Virginia City and neither am I."

There's nothing more for me to do. I head for the ornate hotels on Montgomery, determined to find a Touchstone and get back to Malcolm. I miss him. And I need his cool head to help me figure all this out. Surely one of the hotels with columns and sculptures and gilt-painted ornaments will have a Touchstone among all the architectural details and doodads. The first hotels I try are a bust, but then I come to the fanciest place of all.

The Lick House isn't a house at all, but a grand hotel. I walk into the lobby, decorated with gilt mirrors and potted ferns. It's so fancy, I could be back in London, at the writers' reception where I met Arthur Conan Doyle. Suddenly, I'm all too aware of my dirty dress, my unwashed hair, the stale smell of stable. I don't belong in such a ritzy place.

I hear it before I see it, the trickling fountain in the center of the colonnaded lobby, a marble basin with a merman and conch shells, like a cartoon version of the fountains I'd seen in Rome.

The marble glows with a purple light. Despite how ugly and

tacky it is, the fountain's a Touchstone. I feel a surge of triumph. I did it – I found my ticket home! I hurry to touch it before I get kicked out for looking like a street person. I crouch down and stretch my hand out toward the basin. Just as my fingers settle on the cold stone, I notice the woman sitting on a settee nearby. It's Mom!

I pull back my hand, trying to push myself away from the waves of light glowing brighter and brighter from the fountain. For a second, I think I've escaped the Touchstone's hold as the room freezes around me. I can see Mom looking at me. Then shadows flit across the room, darkness and light swooping in. Mom's face shrinks into a tiny pinprick as the familiar whirl of colors and lights folds me up and spins me around.

July 15

When the world has settled around me again, I'm back in modern day San Francisco, teetering on the sidewalk. I'm outside, on Montgomery Street, the roar of the city all around me as cars rumble by and people shoulder their way past me. The bright colors of store windows and cars and people's clothes seem harsh after the muted colors of the past. Then there were no neon signs. No bright orange or pink. I'm struck by how much artificial color and noise we surround ourselves with, things so much a part of our lives, we don't even notice them.

To my right I see Lotta's Fountain. Across the street is the cafe where Malcolm should be.

I wait anxiously for the light to change, then run to the cafe. It feels good to be back in my right time, to be wearing comfortable jeans and shoes, but my stomach roils with nerves. I need to find my brother.

I scan the dark interior and my heart pounds when I see him. Malcolm sits hunched over his laptop with earbuds on. I've never seen anything so beautiful – my stupid, critical, know-it-all brother! I grab him around the shoulders, leaning in for a tight hug.

He sits up, startled, takes out the earbuds and glares at me.

"Mira! Where's Mom? She's not with you?"

I explain things as clearly as I can, but the more I talk, the more Malcolm smolders. Until finally he erupts.

"You weren't supposed to come back without Mom! Period. Instead you got distracted, having fun chatting with Mark Twain."

"I did not!" My cheeks feel hot because of course it was fun meeting Mark Twain. But I was still looking for Mom.

"Please, Malcolm, let's not fight," I beg. "I know you'd be better at all this than me. I came back because I need your help. Can't you just listen? Please?"

Malcolm slumps in his chair, arms crossed, chin down, his whole body radiating how mad he is. But he's not yelling, so I take his silence as a yes. There were so many things I wanted to ask him, so many things I wanted to check, that now that I'm here, I'm not sure what to do first. I get out my sketchbook, scanning my notes and drawings for reminders.

"So here's what I need to know – what's the change Mom

wanted? Was it getting Mark Twain to write the story about the Chinese laundryman or getting him to sign it with his pen name? And why does the change matter and what does it mean about the future?"

"You're asking the wrong questions. I thought we'd decided that you shouldn't do anything to try to change the future, even if it seems like the right thing to do." Malcolm grabs the sketchbook and leafs through it. "You're supposed to convince Mom of that. Clearly you didn't. Again."

I wince.

He glares at me. "No matter what the horrible thing in the future is, it would be incredibly selfish for us to do something about it in the past. You said so yourself – the only way to change your future is for you to do it. In your right time!"

"I'm sorry," I mumble. "It's just that whenever I see Mom, she's so sure of herself."

"You mean, whenever you see her, you want to make her happy. Well, stop that!" Malcolm snaps. He starts typing quickly into his laptop, which I take as a sign that he's forgiven me, at least enough to help. As he scans the screen, his shoulders soften. He's caught up in whatever he's found. Another good sign.

"Hey, it's interesting about that newspaper story that the *Call* refused to print. From what I see, that changed Mark Twain's mind about journalism. His heart wasn't in it anymore. Here's what he said in his autobiography: 'I was loftier forty years ago than I am now and I felt deep shame in being situated as I was – slave of such a journal as the *Morning Call*. If I had been still loftier I would have thrown up my berth and gone out and starved, like any other hero. But I had never had any experience. I had dreamed heroism, like everybody, but I had no practice and I didn't know how to begin. I couldn't bear to begin by starving . . . Therefore I swallowed my humiliation and stayed where I was, but I took not the least interest in it, and naturally there were results.' The 'results' means that he left his job. Quit before he could be fired. Then he wrote for that other paper you mentioned, the *Alta California,* but he could barely scrape together a living."

"It's funny to hear you read him because now I can hear his voice. That's just how he sounds."

"Lucky you that you know that." Malcolm's voice takes on a hard edge again.

"Can we please not argue anymore?"

"I'm not," Malcolm argues.

"Maybe Mom wanted Twain to become a hard-hitting journalist, exposing corruption, changing the way people think about issues. Not that I'm saying we should change anything. I'm just trying to understand."

"Fom his own description, Twain was about as far as you could get from a driven, idealistic crusader. Although . . ." Malcolm leans closer to the computer screen. "Well, what do you know! The first novel Twain wrote wasn't *Tom Sawyer*. It was *The Gilded Age:*

A Tale of Today, something he co-wrote with another author. It's the story of crooked land speculators, bankers, and politicians. Exactly the kind of muckraking writing you're talking about. You know, humor can be an effective tool for political or social change." Malcolm talks faster, the way he does when an idea excites him. "That's what satire can do. Sometimes it's way more powerful than protests."

"I suppose." I've only read *Tom Sawyer* and that didn't seem like satire.

"I know what you're thinking – there's so much criticism of Twain for being racist." Which isn't what I'm thinking at all, but Malcolm's on his soapbox now and nothing can stop him. "You have to read him in historical context. Yeah, he used the 'n' word, but that's what people said back then. He couldn't invent a language he didn't have. He made Jim a sympathetic character. Plus he helped African-American students pay for college and raised funds for Booker T. Washington's Tuskegee Institute."

"You don't have to prove it to me." Maybe I don't know as much as my brother, but I'm the one who actually met Clemens.

"I'm just saying Twain's writings matter the way they are. He described Americans as close-minded and ignorant in *The Innocents Abroad,* but he made fun of himself as much as everyone else, so he didn't come off as mean. You know, I've tried to do that kind of thing myself with short satirical pieces for the *Jacket.*"

I'm beginning to see a connection. The first time I

time-traveled, it was to Paris and Mom wanted me to convince Zola to write his newspaper article exposing the horrific injustice of the Dreyfus affair. Then in 17th century Rome, Mom wanted us to rescue Giordano Bruno, who was also a powerful writer. Not satire, but philosophy, science, religious thinking. Except last time, in World War I London, I was supposed to make sure a coded message got into the right hands. I can't tell how that fits the pattern.

"Maybe Mom wants to protect free speech. It's not just about intolerance and injustice, but how to fight them with the strongest tools there are. Words." I feel that clarity that strikes when the pieces finally fall into place the way they're supposed to.

"Could be." Malcolm nods thoughtfully. "Writing is a powerful way to fight injustice, reaching as many people as possible." Malcolm leans back smugly. "All the more reason Mom shouldn't risk mucking with the past. It's not about events. It's about attitudes! Ideas! Information!"

"So that's what I tell her? That we'll protect free speech here, today? Will that convince her to come home?"

Malcolm shakes his head. "No, she has to come home for the same reasons we said before. Anyway, Mira, the Inquisition is over."

But as he says it, I realize that's not true. It's just taken a different form now. "There's always censorship. And there are people willing to kill to keep other people from expressing their ideas. There was that attack on that satirical newspaper in Paris, remember?

Those were cartoonists and they were seen as a threat!"

"Good thing I can't draw then." Malcolm hands me back my sketchbook.

"What if that's what happens? You and I, we write or draw something satirical, and some crazy person takes offense . . . and kills us. That could be the connection between what Mom's trying to change and us. Not that we should go along with her!" I think about all the people I've met in the past. "Zola was convicted of libel for his writing and ended up killed. Bruno was condemned by the Inquisition. But Mark Twain didn't suffer for his writing. He became world famous!"

"Yeah, but he's often censored today. How many schools don't allow their students to read *Tom Sawyer?* How many teachers present him as an ugly racist? There's a different kind of censorship, the kind done in the name of caring."

"That makes no sense!"

"It's like when colleges restrict books or speakers, worried that students will be hurt or offended." Malcolm shudders. "It's a smarmy, self-righteous censorship that swaddles people in a cozy, feel-good place where they'll never face a disturbing idea."

"I hate it when grown-ups act as if kids can't handle controversy. Really we're so much better at it than adults."

"So you agree – no changes, no matter what! Mom has to treat us like responsible people, not babies that have to be coddled."

I nod. "This time I'll do it, I promise. How about coming with me to Lotta's Fountain? You must be sick of sitting here."

"Yeah, okay." Malcom turns off the laptop and stuffs it into his messenger bag. "But let's take a little detour before you go back in time. I've been looking online for historical bits of the city."

Malcolm leads the way along Montgomery, zigzagging on Sutter and then over to California, pointing out buildings that date back to the early 1900s.

The oldest remnant is near the top of Nob Hill, at the corner of Sacramento and Taylor. "See this bit of the sidewalk. It's from 1871. And if we go a little further . . ."

It's actually a lot further, especially when you consider the steep hills, but at 1032 Broadway, Malcolm points out a house that was built in 1859, which means it was here when I time-traveled. I imagine I could look in the window and see myself wearing the old-fashioned gingham of 1864.

Around the corner is a small park named after Ina Coolbrith, a person I've never heard of, but who Maclom explains was the first poet laureate of California – and of any U.S. state. The whole idea of a poet laureate was invented here, in San Francisco. Malcolm is ready to launch into a long lecture about the literary culture of the city, from early days to Beat Poets and Ginsburg's *Howl,* but he knows he's pushing it. I've humored him long enough and it's time to head back. I haven't forgotten about Mom and neither has he, though he insists on one more stop at the Wells Fargo building, back on Montgomery, where you can see a real stagecoach, gold and silver ingots, photos and posters from the days of the Wild West.

I'm eager to finally get things right, but I have to admit it's a great tour of old San Francisco tucked inside the modern city. Funny how you can still see them side by side, if you know where to look. I smile at my brother.

"You've figured out how to time-travel yourself!"

"It's not the same thing at all! First you get to meet Arthur Conan Doyle, now Mark Twain . . ." Malcolm shakes his head. But at least he doesn't sound mad.

We're back at Lotta's Fountain, another piece of the past. It's as ugly as ever, even with the shimmering green and gold lights whirling around it. It looks more powerful than before. Can

Touchstones change? This one looks like it has somehow.

"You'll be okay, won't you?" I ask Malcolm.

"I haven't written anything that's worth censoring yet."

He tips up his chin and steps back. "Just promise me you'll stay strong and stand up to Mom. Tell her she's suffocating us. We need to be free to think for ourselves, to make our own mistakes, to decide our own futures."

I nod, determined not to let him down this time. I touch the fountain and the world topples around me, lights flickering and spinning, the earth shifting beneath me in rolling tremors. A dizzying rush of lights, colors, and then inky darkness wraps all around me.

October 2, 1866

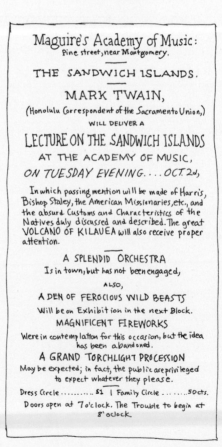

Maguire's Academy of Music:
Pine street, near Montgomery.

THE SANDWICH ISLANDS.

MARK TWAIN,
(Honolulu Correspondent of the Sacramento Union,)
WILL DELIVER A

LECTURE ON THE SANDWICH ISLANDS
AT THE ACADEMY OF MUSIC,
ON TUESDAY EVENING.... OCT. 2d,

In which passing mention will be made of Harris,
Bishop Staley, the American Missionaries, etc., and
the absurd Customs and Characteristics of the
Natives duly discussed and described. The great
VOLCANO OF KILAUEA will also receive proper
attention.

A SPLENDID ORCHESTRA
Is in town, but has not been engaged,

ALSO,

A DEN OF FEROCIOUS WILD BEASTS
Will be on Exhibition in the next Block.
MAGNIFICENT FIREWORKS
Were in contemplation for this occasion, but the idea
has been abandoned.
A GRAND TORCHLIGHT PROCESSION
May be expected; in fact, the public are privileged
to expect whatever they please.

Dress Circle .... $1 | Family Circle .... 50 cts.

Doors open at 7 o'clock. The Trouble to begin at
8 o'clock

I know the date right away because the first thing I see is a poster with the words "Tonight!" emblazoned across the top. The poster leans against the entrance of the Academy of Music, one of the theaters I'd gone to for reviews. Only the performance advertised for tonight isn't a concert or play. It's a lecture. By none other than Mark Twain – yes, that's the name on the billboard, not Sam Clemens.

So Mark Twain is still a reporter! Only now he works for the *Sacramento Union*. I thought he'd turn to writing the kinds of stories he enjoyed, funny tall tales. Though it's clear from the poster he's still using that deadpan humor, even as a journalist. Maybe especially as one. The poster is like a page from *Mad* magazine. Satire again!

I must be here in this time to see him. Which means Mom might be at the lecture tonight. Another reason to go. Normally the word "lecture" means "prepare to be bored," but with all the silly promises of what won't be involved, from fireworks to ferocious beasts, I'm betting it will be more like a stand-up comedy act than a serious talk. Plus this is Mark Twain speaking – it's going to be great!

From the position of the sun, I'm guessing it's around three o'clock, so I have some time before the doors open at seven. Enough time to figure out how to scrounge up the fifty cents I'll need for a ticket.

I know just who to borrow the money from. I head to the *Call* offices, still in the same building, still on the third floor, and there still setting type, is Scout. The same face, the same shoulders, the same hair. I want to hug him, but instead I stand there, waiting for him to look up from his work. A few minutes pass and I can't wait any longer. I give a fake cough.

"Miss Lodge!" he yelps, startled. "You're back!"

"Just for a little while," I say. "I saw the sign advertising Clemens' talk about the Sandwich Islands. Looks like my timing is perfect."

This is an era when people come and go and nobody thinks twice about it, so he doesn't grill me about why I left so abruptly. That was tricky in the other places I time-traveled, but seems part of normal life in the West. So is wearing the same clothes forever, so if Scout notices that my dress is the same old gingham, he doesn't mention it.

But I have my own questions, like when did Clemens change jobs? Does he live in Sacramento now? Did his friend follow him? "Where's Steve Gillis, the typesetter?" I ask first.

"You haven't heard?" Scout shakes his head. "That's right, you left before that whole mess."

He sets down the box of type and leans back while he tells me the whole convoluted story. One drunken night, Gillis hit a saloonkeeper on the head with a pitcher of beer and almost killed him. Who knew that assault with beer could be so dangerous? Anyway, Clemens paid the high bail, $500, but Gillis decided to skip town, heading back to the Sierra foothills. He told Clemens what he was doing, and the two left together. Clemens was $500 poorer, but one friend richer.

"And that stay with Gillis out in Jackass Hill turned out to be a great investment because that's where he wrote the story that's made him so famous," Scout finishes.

"Clemens is famous?" Already? Surely, he hasn't written *Tom Sawyer* yet. He seems too young. Plus he's still a reporter.

"Well, Clemens ain't, but Mark Twain is. That's how he signed *Jim Smiley and His Jumping Frog*. He can tell you the whole thing himself, how he came back to San Francisco, leaving Steve out there in mining territory, found a letter here from an old friend, Artemus Ward, I think his name was. The letter was asking for a story to include in an upcoming book. Clemens sent in the frog story, which he'd written while out in Jackass Hill. You can take Clemens away from the paper, but you can't keep the fellow from writing! It's like his natural element." Scout rummages through some papers on the desk, finds a newspaper with a lot more pages than the *Call*, and hands it to me. It's *The New York Saturday Press*, and the date is November 18, 1865, the price six cents. Right there on the first page is Mark Twain's byline on a story that starts out as a letter to his friend, Artemus Ward.

"Anyway, Clemens didn't know that by the time he got the letter, the book had already come out, so instead Ward's publisher passed on the frog story to this fancy New York newspaper. Mark Twain is now a big name. Got him that cushy assignment to go to the Sandwich Islands and write up his impressions. I hear he's heading for a big tour of Europe next, all on the newspaper's dime."

I scan the story and realize I know this one, only when I read it, the title was *The Celebrated Jumping Frog of Calaveras County.* In fact, if you go to Angels Camp, an old mining town in the Sierra Foothills, they still have frog jumping contests every spring. It's their big claim to fame. Mom and Dad took us there one year on our way to Yosemite. It's one of those cute towns that look like the setting for a Western.

The year we went, some kid's frog won. I didn't see how you could train a frog to jump. It seemed like a matter of luck. But the boy insisted he'd been training his frog for weeks.

It's funny to think that I'm seeing the start of that tradition, holding it in my hands actually. Not that this is important history, but still, it's cool.

"I'd love to see him again. Clemens, I mean." I hand the newspaper back to Scout and give him my best smile (at least I hope it's a pretty good one). "How about we go together? Your treat?"

Scout blushes to the tips of his ears. "Yeah, of course! I was going anyway, already got my ticket. I'll get one for you and we can go together. Maybe have some supper before?"

I can't stop smiling, for real, thinking that Scout likes me the way I like him. The way I liked all the boys he reminds me of.

"If you want to catch up with Mr. Clemens before the big show tonight, I'm guessing he'll be at the Monkey Building, where all the writers hang out. Come back here at 5 and we'll get something to eat before the trouble starts."

I get the hint. Scout needs to get back to work and I'm distracting him. I like that idea. "See you tonight!" I sing out as I leave.

I remember Clemens pointing out the Monkey Building to me, a big square brick block. As I walk up Montgomery, I realize I was right, it's exactly where the Transamerica Pyramid stands today. It's so freaky seeing San Francisco in these historical layers, the past on top of the present and the present on top of the past.

Now as I walk up the street, instead of bustling bankers or ambling tourists, chickens and turkeys cross the road. To get to the other side, of course. Goats and sheep graze together in yards next to houses. I could be out in the country, except the houses are closer  together. And trams pulled by horses trundle along nearby.

I'm not sure where to go in the Monkey Building. I figure I'll ask whoever I see if they know where Sam Clemens is. But as soon as I'm inside, I hear the murmur of voices and follow the sound to a room filled with chairs and desks and people. Most are men, but

I'm surprised to see a couple of women as well. In the back of the room, facing everyone else, stand two men. I recognize Bret Harte from the description Clemens gave of him on that long-ago ride to the Cliff House. And right next to him is Clemens himself.

Naturally, Clemens is the one talking. "By now I'm sure you've all heard the story of my return to San Francisco and my desperate scheme to make money by giving a public lecture. An obvious solution to my poverty, surely, for who doesn't want to hear a man talk about experiences they can only imagine. No one, you say? People aren't interested in volcanoes or hula dancers or sugar plantations? That's probably true, but I found a kind soul who remembered me from my days reviewing his spectacles and he offered me his fine theater, Maguire's Academy of Music, for half price – fifty dollars. So I began with that sizeable investment in my own speech. I've staked more than that since you could have a brilliant play by the great bard himself, but if nobody knows about it, nobody will come. Which means I spent another hundred and fifty dollars to print fliers and advertise all over town.

"So now, I'm poorer than ever, more desperate than ever. And only you, my good friends, can save me. I wrote on the posters that the trouble will begin at eight, but I don't mean that's when I want tomatoes thrown in my face. I want side-splitting laughter to erupt and that's where I rely on you."

There are a few forced chuckles, but Clemens ignores them.

"Now I expect you to choose seats all over the auditorium and to laugh loudly whenever I say something funny. That should prompt the folks around you to laugh as well, because nobody wants to be left out of a joke. They'll chuckle just to make it seem like they got the point. If you're not sure whether it's a joke, I'll wink, and those of you in the front rows can start peals of laughter that can travel all the way to the back."

"Do you really need us for that?" a tall woman asks. "Have more faith in your sense of humor, Sam." The woman is elegant and beautiful. Is she a writer, too?

"My humor comes off well on the printed page. I'm just not sure how it works in the spoken form. Especially when I'm the one doing the speaking. Now you must understand the difference here between comic, humorous, and witty. Witty is for the French and it involves word play and clever turns of thought, and that lowest form of humor, the dreaded pun. That, as you can imagine, is not my style – no cleverness for me, if you please! Comic stories are more English – the teller is sure he's telling you the funniest thing in the world. He's laughing himself before you even begin to titter. If you laugh at all, it's because he's bludgeoned you into doing so. That also is not my style.

"I belong – or aspire to belong – to the illustruous line of American humorists. And here is the difference – the humorist acts as if the absurd thing he's describing isn't funny at all, which, of course, only makes it more hilarious. That is my model. Which means, I'm trying to be funniest when you think I'm most grave. When I speak like a professor, I'm really being a comic. So please, laugh accordingly! And don't forget to applaud loudly when I'm introduced and at the end when I'm finished."

"Don't worry, Sam. We'll clap you off the stage," Harte assures him.

"Most important of all, invite all your friends, strangers, enemies. Buy them tickets if you must. If I have to face empty seats, my throat will dry up, my hands will shake, my legs will tremble. The lecture will end before it begins! My fate, my dear friends, my pocketbook, is in your hands."

Harte starts clapping, as if to prove how well he'll do tonight, and everyone in the room joins in. Me, too. We're all telling Clemens that he'll do fine tonight, better than fine.

Clemens bows dramatically, sweeping his arms wide. "Do this tonight and I'll stand you all drinks tomorrow!"

"And if you believe that," Harte quips, "Then I have a silver mine to sell you!"

The meeting, if that's what it is, seems to be over. People

cluster in small groups or leave. I walk up to Clemens, who's talking with the tall woman.

"Mr. Clemens! I'm glad to see you back in San Francisco. Scout told me about your adventures and your great success with the *Jumping Frog* story."

"It's Miss Lodge, isn't it? I never forget a face, but I often lose names. Yours, however, seems to have stayed with me." Clemens smiles. "Lodged in my brain, as it were. And this is Miss Coolbrith, a talented poet who works with the equally talented Bret Harte."

I almost make a crack about puns and how Clemens is more French than he knows, but I catch myself. Instead I say something just as stupid – "I didn't know there were any women poets these days!" Especially as I feel a memory nudge itself forward. Coolbrith! That was the name of the park Malcolm showed me, the one named for the first Californian – and American – poet laureate.

Luckily, Miss Coolbrith doesn't look offended. "There aren't many. But I've always loved books. I feel more at home with them than with people."

"I would love to read your work." I gush to make up for putting my foot in my mouth.

"And so you must! Miss Coolbrith should be the one giving this lecture. She's quite the public speaker, as enchanting in person as she is on paper." Clemens winks.

Miss Coolbrith blushes. "I haven't your wit! After tonight, your reputation as a humorist will surpass Artemus Ward's."

"Ah, you think my frog will outjump his? I surely hope so!"

I turn to Clemens, feeling like I'm interrupting a flirtatious dance. "I'm curious how you started writing for the Sacramento paper. I heard you left the *Call,* so I thought you'd given up reporting entirely."

"For a while reporting gave up on me! I tried writing for the *Alta California,* Bret's journal, but I earned so little, I was ashamed to see my friends. Even worse was seeing my landlady. It was a low period in a lowly life, so when I left with my friend Steve Gillis, I thought I'd start over. That's what the great West offers, you know — as many new beginnings as you like. You can re-invent yourself over and over again until you find a face that works for you. So I used that name I'd coined before, Mark Twain, and set it on a trifling story, a merry piece of fluff I'd written about life in Angels Camp. And the rest is history!"

"I'm glad to see you doing so well! And I can't wait to hear your talk tonight." I love the idea of reinventing myself. I can be a braver Miriam Lodge now than I was before.

"You'll be there?" Clemens tips back on his heels, grinning widely. "Another person to laugh at my slender jokes and applaud wildly at the end?"

"Definitely!" I promise. "I'm going with Scout. He's getting me a ticket."

"Do I smell romance in the air?" Clemens teases.

I feel my cheeks heat up. "What about yourself?"

Clemens barks out a delighted laugh. "If Miss Coolbrith

would have me, I'd be forever hers, but I know better than to presume such favor."

Miss Coolbrith arches an elegant eyebrow. "I'm afraid I've pledged myself to poetry. I'd rather that verse should own me than any man. I'll see you both tonight then." The woman bows her head and glides away.

"Well, I must prepare for tonight. I think a good, long nap is in order, don't you?"

"I'm glad I got a last chance to talk with you. I loved your frog story! I can't wait to see what other things you write." Once again I wonder if he's a time-traveler, too, like Arthur Conan Doyle, but he doesn't write any science fiction type stuff. Except! I stifle a gasp.

"Are you alright, my dear? You look like you've seen a ghost all of a sudden."

"I just remembered something, that's all," I babble. A book, that is, one that Mark Twain writes later. And it's about time-travel! "I thought of that English writer, the one who writes about time-travel, and I wondered if you'd ever read his work." But he can't have read H.G. Wells – he's only just been born probably. He definitely hasn't written anything yet. Did anybody else write about time-travel this early? Mark Twain can't have been the first. If he is, that must mean something! Wait, there are the ghosts of the past, present, and future from Dickens' *A Christmas Carol*, but that's not really time-travel, not the way I'm thinking of, not the way Mark Twain wrote about.

"I don't know anyone who writes about time-travel. You mean going back into the past or visiting the future?" Clemens looks intrigued. "It's an interesting idea. Yes, that could make a wonderfully humorous story. Now if I wrote about something like that, I'd have my hero go back to King Arthur's Court, to a time of knights and ladies and courtly adventure. You can just imagine how a rough miner would deal with a suit of armor!"

I gulp. That's exactly what he will write about, only it won't be a western miner, but a New England farmer, and the book will be *A Connecticut Yankee in King Arthur's Court*. Did I just make this story happen by suggesting the idea of time-travel? Suddenly every word I say seems risky.

"Whatever you write will be wonderfully funny," I gush awkwardly. "I should let you rest now. See you tonight!" I turn to go, wondering what damage I might have caused. Every step seems treacherous. I need to bring Mom home and get out of here as soon as I can.

I leave the building, wondering where Mom could be. I don't have any ideas, so I do the same thing I'd do in my own time, walk toward the water, seeking out a soothing view of the bay.

A ship is lodged between two buildings, a ladder leaning against its side for easy entry. It's a real ship, but a hotel sits on its deck. On the other side of the building next to it, there's another ship, this one with a store built on top. And the building between the two ships has a mast coming out of its roof, as if it swallowed another ship. How did they end up stranded on land like this? It's a surreal image, like something you'd see in a dream.

People are coming and going into the boats as if they were regular businesses. Could this be where Mom's staying? I follow a woman carrying loaves of bread in a basket up the stairs to the Niantic Boat Hotel.

The lobby looks like a regular hotel, just smaller.

"What kind of room would you like, Miss?" the desk clerk asks.

"Actually, I'm looking for a friend who said she'd be here." I show the man the sketch of Mom.

He shakes his head. "No, not here. Are you sure she's at the Niantic?"

"She didn't mention the name, but aren't you the only hotel

built on a boat?"

"That's our claim to fame, alright. Not that sleeping on a boat appeals to many folks. But we had to do something with it, so why not a hotel? Better than the ship that got turned into a jail."

"I must have misunderstood her then." I tuck away my sketchbook. "So how did this get built? Why abandon a ship? And how did you drag it onto land? That can't have been easy!"

The clerk snorts out a laugh. "Nobody did that! The water around the docks got filled in. Some smart fellers used the sandy hills to fill in the waterfront. Added a good extra bit past Montgomery. That used to be the edge of the city."

"And the ship owners weren't mad that their boats got land-locked that way?"

"Maybe, but not much they could do about it. A lot of boats were abandoned here as soon their crews arrived in the 1850s. Everyone headed to the hills for gold. Much more profitable than being a sailor!"

Was this something Malcolm told me about? It sounds familiar. But he's told me so many facts, they seem to spill right out of my head. I can't call them up the way he can.

It's odd to be on a boat that feels so solid, no rocking waves beneath. I climb back down the ladder, standing on ground that was bay water not that long ago. Between the buildings, I can see real boats on actual water.

It's my familiar bay, the one I love to look at from our roof.

From here, it's still pretty, but somehow expressionless, like a face without eyebrows. Without the Golden Gate or the Bay Bridge, the water is flat and empty.

It's a clear, crisp day. So clear, I can see the buildings on Alcatraz. There's a squat lighthouse and some low white structures.

 Oh yeah, there was a fort there before the prison. Soldiers must still be stationed there. And the lower levels were used for prisoners during the Civil War. That's right, Clemens had written a story about a general giving a grand tour to a bunch of officials. He'd mentioned Ft. Point and Alcatraces.

Seeing San Francisco like this, as it was and as it will be, I feel more connected to this place than ever, like time is stitching me to it through different layers of cloth. Maybe this is the true magic of time-travel, knowing a place as it shifts and changes, feeling a deeper connection to it. I know I should be thinking about Mom. But right now, I'm grateful for this here, this now.

The shadows grow longer and it's time to meet Scout for dinner. I head back to the *Call* offices, nervously combing my fingers through my hair.

Scout has changed into clean clothes, his hair slicked back with water. He's trying to look nice for me and I feel more self-conscious than ever. Which makes conversation suddenly horribly awkward. We walk to the restaurant Scout's chosen, not sure what to say to each other.

The only safe subject is Sam Clemens or Steve Gillis, the people we have in common. So I try that.

"Have you heard from Steve since he went back to mining?" I ask.

"He's not mining. He's back working at the *Enterprise* in Virginia City. There's more steady cash in handling lead type than digging for gold or silver."

"Oh." I search for a new topic. "You know, I remember Clemens telling me that when he first came to San Francisco, it was because he had to leave Virginia City in a hurry. Was he skipping bail then, too?"

Scout laughs, breaking the tension. "He was skipping something alright! He'd written an article poking fun of the editor of another local newspaper and got himself challenged to a duel."

"A duel! That sounds so, I don't know, old-fashioned. Or do you mean those kinds of shoot-outs gunslingers have in front of saloons?" I can't imagine Clemens with a Stetson and a six-shooter.

"No, it was a regular duel, the kind at dawn, twenty paces and all that. A fight for honor, that kind of stupid thing. The duel ended up being cancelled since neither Clemens nor the other editor wanted to risk it. They're writers, not fighters!"

"So why leave then?"

"Because dueling had just been made illegal in Nevada

Territory and a judge warned Clemens he'd be prosecuted to set an example if he didn't leave. So he left."

"But he hadn't actually been in a duel!"

"The judge seemed to consider that a minor detail. Anyway, it wasn't such a bad thing for Clemens to come here. He didn't like the *Call,* it's true, but he loved San Francisco."

I smile, looking around me. "Who doesn't?"

That bit of conversation gets us into the restaurant, a small tavern near the theater. And it breaks the ice, so we can be kind of normal with each other again.

Until dessert, when Scout says, "So what happened with your mother? Did you convince her to come back to your family?"

Something about the way he says it sets me on edge. It's a perfectly harmless question, but somehow it doesn't feel like one. There's a sharpness to his tone.

"Actually, I gave up looking for her. We're fine without her." I chew on the apple pie but the crust has turned from flakey to chalky dust.

"Really? You don't seem like the type to give up." Again, there's that jabbing.

"How do you know what type I am?" I snap.

"I'm sorry!" Scout says, sounding not at all sorry. In fact, he sounds annoyed more than anything. "I said 'you seem,' not that I know anything. I just thought you were more dogged, more determined. Forget I said anything."

Something is definitely wrong. I have the unsettling feeling that Scout is spying on me. Could he be working for the Watcher, trying to find out where Mom is by using me?

Any illusion of a date, of friendship even, has vanished. We'd have an excruciating walk home, except there's no need. The theater is down the street. Scout pays the bill and I thank him profusely. I don't want him to suspect that I'm on to him. So I try to act normal, which, of course, is a recipe for seeming like a complete weirdo.

Clemens was worried the place would be empty except for his friends, but there's a crowd pushing inside when we get there.

"I'm lucky you could get me a ticket. Mark Twain is more popular than he thought!"

"Than anyone thought," Scout says.

There are people in fancy dress with gloves and hats and workers wearing clothes still dirty from the mines or farms or whatever. I catch sight of Ina Coolbrith, whose height stands out in a crowd. If Mom's here, she's so short, it'll be tough to find her. And I can't go near her so long as Scout's nearby. Good thing our seats aren't together!

I remember how Clemens taught me to rate audiences during my brief stint as entertainment reviewer. This audience is a total mix, the kind that only the most popular shows attracted. There's a buzz of excitement and I catch snippets of gossip.

"He used to be a local reporter here, you know!"

"That frog story was a side-splitter, I tell you. If he can talk half as good as he writes, it'll be a rare treat tonight!"

"I've always wanted to go to the Sandwich Islands! So exotic, so primitive, so colorful! To see an actual volcano, just imagine!"

Then I catch a glimpse of another familiar face – it's the

Watcher. Dressed in lilac, with an elegant black hat perched on her head.

I stare at her, waiting to see if she looks at me or Scout, but she's talking to Ina Coolbrith.

I tell Scout that I see someone I know and I'll find him later. He doesn't try to stop me, and for a second I wonder if I'm wrong about him. After all, he reminds so much of those other boys, the ones I liked. Could he really be on the side of the Watcher?

I shove past people, trying to get closer to the patch of purple that winks between the men's suits and the ladies' dresses.

And then she's there, all by herself now and close enough that I can grab her elbow. Which I do.

"What are you doing here?" I hiss. "I told you I'd take care of my mother."

"You said you were leaving!" The Watcher glares at me.

"Give me one last chance! Please!"

The Watcher snorts. "It's always just one more chance with you! This is it then. Your absolute last chance. Either she goes home with you today, from this time, or she never goes home at all."

"I'll convince her," I gulp. "This time I know what to say."

The Watcher's lips curl in disdain. "I hope so. For both of your sakes." Then she plunges back into the mass of bodies and disappears, leaving me shaking.

What had the poster said, doors open at 7, the trouble starts at 8? I feel like the trouble has already started. I've got to find Mom! The crowd swirls around me, thicker than ever. How could Mark Twain draw such a big audience when all he's written is one silly story about a frog?

A gong clangs, signaling people to find their seats and be quiet. The lobby is still full of bodies and it takes forever for the crowd to thin enough so I can find my seat, way in the back. I'll just have to find Mom afterwards. If I wait outside the front door, I won't miss her.

The lights dim, voices hush, and then a spotlight glows on the closed curtains. A man parts them and steps through. It's Clemens – or rather, Mark Twain – though I can barely make out his face, I'm so far away.

Twain steps up to the podium and starts to speak, but I guess microphones haven't been invented yet, because I can barely hear him. His voice is soft and wavery, not the firm drawl I know. He's got stage fright! And looking at the packed sea of faces all turned toward him, I can't blame him. Every seat is filled. Not just those on the ground floor, but in the two rows of balconies as well.

People strain forward, trying to hear. Will someone throw a tomato, like Twain feared? This is going to be a disaster! I wish I could blame the Watcher, but what difference could she make? Public speaking is scary to most people, though I would have guessed Twain has just the right personality for pulling off this kind of talk. I think of all the oral reports my stomach has pitched through and my knees feel shaky in sympathy.

But Twain doesn't give up. He keeps talking and his voice gets louder, firmer. "If there's a horrible malady in the world, it's stage fright, and I admit to suffering a brief bout of that myself today. It reminds me of another terrible illness, sea-sickness. I've only been sea-sick once, on a little ship near the Sandwich Islands. It may have only been that one time, but I was so sick, there wasn't any left for the other passengers." And just like that, he's launched

into his talk, moving smoothly on to his adventures in the Sandwich Islands.

I remember what he said back in the Monkey Building, about the difference between being witty, comic, and humorous. This is definitely Humorous, with a capital H. Twain's so wonderfully dry and funny, I laugh myself hoarse. I clap until my hands hurt. I forget all about the Watcher, Mom, time-travel, anything until the lights go up and the room is filled with thunderous applause.

I feel wonderfully light. Nothing can go wrong after so much laughter.

I wait outside the entrance, scouring the people as they leave for Mom's familiar face. The tall poet walks by and gives me a nod. Scout sees me and comes over, a big smile lighting up his face.

"Wasn't that something? I'm sorry we couldn't sit together, but the main thing was seeing Mr. Clemens! Would you like to join us at the Lick House? Everyone's meeting for a celebratory drink there."

I would love to congratulate Clemens, to tell him how funny he was. But seeing Mom is more important.

"You go on ahead," I say. "I'll come by later if I can."

"Well, of course, you can. It's whether you will!" But Scout doesn't press and his voice is cheery, not sharp. Maybe I imagined the whole thing over dinner.

I keep my eyes focused on the door, intent on not missing anyone. I see tall people, short people, fancy people, plain people, and then finally, the one person I'm looking for.

"Mom!" I grab her arm before she can run. Anyway, the street is too crowded for anyone to move quickly. "I talked to Malcolm and he agrees – you need to come home. Let us take care of ourselves."

Mom frowns. "I told you, you don't understand! Neither of you do!"

"Then explain it to me!" I grab both arms now, forcing her to face me. "You're as bad as the Watcher, trying to control people. Let me take my own risks, make my own choices! I'm not helping you anymore and you can't do this without me!"

Mom lowers her eyes, her body slumping. Then she nods, slowly. "You're right. Walk with me and I'll explain . . . everything." We head uphill, away from the crowds of people still milling around the front of the theater. I can't believe it – after all this time, she's finally trusting me! I can feel the nervous energy radiating from her wiry muscles. Whatever she's going to tell me, it's got to be big.

"The reason I've been going back in time has been to fix things, to put things right."

"I know," I say, disappointed that there's nothing else to this.

"No, you think we've been trying to change history. But what we've really been doing is fixing history, changing things back to how they're supposed to be."

"What do you mean? Why would they need fixing? Does

time just fracture like that?"

"It's the Watcher. Yes, she's chasing me, but only because I've been chasing her. I'm a Watcher, too, Mira." Mom looks at me, waiting for me to take in what she's saying. "And she's a rogue Watcher, a Watcher gone bad."

I'm so stunned, I step back from her. "You're one of the people who police time-travelers?! Since when?"

Mom folds her arms across her chest calmly. "Since a long time. I 'retired' once you kids were born. It all seemed too risky. I was called out of retirement because of Vera – that's the Watcher."

I've never heard the Watcher's real name before. Somehow it makes her seem less dangerous, more human. "What happened with Vera? How is she a problem?"

Mom sighs. She looks and sounds just like my mother, tucking a stray strand of hair behind her ear. She doesn't seem like a Watcher at all.

"Vera was one of our best Watchers, powerful, smart, experienced. She time-traveled a lot, saw a lot of history being made. Something happened, I don't know what, that made her feel like she knew better than everyone else how things should happen. She thought that the only way to make the world a peaceful place was to censor people, to control their thoughts."

I'm still trying to wrap my mind around the idea that Mom is a Watcher, the good kind (there's a good kind?), and the Watcher is the bad guy here.

"She believes that all that matters is that people be fed, housed, clothed. They don't need ideas, they don't need freedom of expression, especially since that expression can lead to violent conflicts as different ideologies clash." Mom sounds sad, not angry.

"So every time we've gone into the past, it's been to fix something Vera has tried to change?" When I think about how many times the Watcher yelled at me for not just observing! What a hypocrite!

"Yes, and it all has to do with the power of language, of words, to influence people. In her mind censorship is good, it protects people. She thinks she's saving humanity from itself." Mom shakes her head. "She's become a fanatic in her rigid beliefs."

"That's awful!" So the Watcher has been the censor Mom's been working against. Malcolm was more right than he knew. "You mean Vera causes the Horrible Thing in the future?"

"I'm trying to save all of us from Vera, to put things right." Mom hesitates. She's not looking me in the eyes now and that makes me think she's about to lie. Is she going to do some of her own censoring-in-the-name-of-protection?

I don't say anything. I wait.

"And you. Yes, you and Malcolm, too. It's personal with us. Because you're next on her list. You've probably guessed that she was trying to stop Clemens from writing, especially from writing satire. Vera considers that the most damaging kind of expression. The pen is mightier than the sword and tyrants know this. That's why they try to keep their people ignorant and unquestioning."

Mom has no idea how much she sounds like Malcolm right now. "Are you saying I'm going to be a writer? Or Malcolm is?"

"I can't reveal your future to you, so don't ask! But stopping the Watcher isn't just about saving you."

"How do I know you're telling me the truth now? I don't want to change things in the past just to help me. You have to trust me to take care of myself! You can't swaddle me in blankets the way Vera wants to do with the entire planet."

Mom winces, but she doesn't give up. "We still have to stop the Watcher, both of us, together," she insists.

I want to say yes, to do what she asks. But I need to know more. I have to understand this better or I'll be choosing blindly, just like Malcolm warned me not to do.

"If this isn't really about my future, why do you need me? I mean, of course I want to stop a Watcher who's changing the past because that's plain wrong. But why me?"

"Because Vera is powerful, very powerful. You and I, since we're related, have a special power, too. But it hasn't been enough so far. Which is why now we have to face her together."

"Because this is our last chance? Doyle said the whole point of time-travel is that you always have more time than you think."

"Yes and no. Vera is getting stronger and soon there will be no way to stop her. She feeds on the rifts she creates in time, gaining power with each one. Even when we undo or correct it, she's gotten a kind of charge out of it. Remember how each time you resisted a

Touchstone in the British Museum, each time you didn't touch one of those powerful objects, you ended up feeling stronger? It's the same thing."

I gape at Mom. How did she know about the British Museum? She wasn't with me.

"There's a connection between time-travelers, Touchstones, and time itself. We're all part of the same fabric. We're all linked. I thought Vera would be at Mark Twain's talk, but I didn't see her there. Which means we have to find her now." Mom sounds more urgent than ever.

"I saw her at the theater, but she didn't do anything."

"It's too late now for her to change Mark Twain. He'll become the brilliant writer he's meant to be."

"She wanted to change that?" I feel sick to my stomach.

"She'll have moved on, to her next chance. That's the 1906 earthquake."

Malcolm's right again! Now that's a spooky talent, more mysterious than time-travel or making Touchstones.

"Remember the vegetable cart the Watcher tipped over? She was trying to ruin Luigi Giannini, the beginning of his business, a fruit-and-vegetable business that will turn into a successful bank – after the earthquake." Mom's calmer now, back in her familiar lecturing mode. Again I wonder, is she really a Watcher?

I shake my head. It's too much, way too much. First Mom wouldn't tell me anything. Now she's saying more than I can understand.

I don't get what a vegetable cart has to do with a bank has to do with censorship has to do with the Watcher.

"I'll explain later. Right now we each need to find a Touchstone. Separately. We can't touch the same one at the same time. Not yet. Go back to the *Call* offices. You'll find a Touchstone there. I'll see you in a few decades." Mom pulls me to her for a tight hug. Which isn't like Mom at all. Now she's really scaring me, but I'm relieved to feel her arms around me, to smell her familiar scent of lavender and freshly-washed cotton.

Then she lets go and is gone. I'm left alone at the top of a small hill, what someday will be Potrero Hill, looking down into the city where a few lights still flicker. Behind me are fields and farms. Not a hint of the city that will be here. It all seems so tenuous now, as if the Watcher could erase it all.

As I walk to the *Call* building, I sift through everything Mom said. It makes sense, in a jumbled sort of way. The Watcher is really a fanatic, and that's what makes her so dangerous. I wonder what time she's really from, where she grew up, what she believed in as a child. Maybe someplace really unstable so that security is more important to her than anything else.

I hope the newspaper office will still be open, and, of course, it is. Scout and the typesetter must be hard at work, printing up the next morning's edition. I'm betting there will be a glowing review of Twain's lecture.

"You're here!" Scout greets me when I come in. He's good at acting normal. "We missed you at the celebration."

"I'm sure nobody noticed I wasn't there," I say, as I look around the room for a Touchstone.

"I noticed!"

"You're the only one. Anyway, was Mr. Clemens happy with how it all went? He must have been!"

"He was tickled! He said he felt like he'd found his true calling, spinning stories, both on paper and out loud. He has a gift as a humorist, a true talent. I wish there was something I was meant to do like that. Setting type, that's a job. Not a calling."

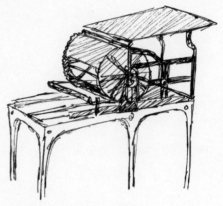

"Since you're here, girly, can you go around the corner and fetch us some beers? Setting type may not be a calling, but it's thirsty work." A man with a pug nose and bald head looks up from the rows of type. He must be Steve Gillis' replacement. And not a pleasant one.

"Lucas, this is Miss Lodge. She used to work here as a reporter. She's not a barmaid to fetch and carry for you."

"Well, since she's not a reporter now, why's she here?"

Scout's cheeks flame bright red. "I imagine to see me! We

had supper together tonight."

"Well lah-di-dah for you two, then!" Lucas throws off his apron and shoves past me to the door. "I need a break to wet my whistle. You can finish without me." He doesn't wait for a response, just stomps off.

"He must be awful to work with!" I blurt out.

"He's not exactly a peach. But it's hard to find a skilled man who'll stay. The gold and silver mines still tempt fellows."

"Not you?"

Scout shakes his head. "I like living in San Francisco."

I wonder what could be a Touchstone here and how I could have missed it before. Unless it's something new – that makes sense. The problem is, once I find it, how do I disappear right in front of Scout? I've got to get rid of him somehow. Or wait until he leaves.

"If you want to join Lucas, go ahead. I'll wait here for you."

"Are you trying to get rid of me?"

Now it's my turn to blush. "Of course not! I'm trying to be nice."

I look around the room, anywhere but at Scout, and there, in the corner, is an old typewriter, different from the one Clemens used. It's glowing silver-green, bristling with power like a Touchstone. An actual portable Touchstone, though not one small enough to slip into a pocket.

I walk towards it, but I can't vanish into thin air. I've got to get Scout of here.

"You are nice." Scout slips between me and the typewriter,

leaning in close. He's not going to kiss me, is he? Why is he acting this way? Why now all of a sudden?

I whip my head to the side and his lips graze my ear.

Scout pulls back, his face red.

"Sorry!"

"No, I'm sorry!" What I really am is suspicious. He wasn't like this before, not when I wanted him to be. "Maybe you should go," I suggest.

"But I work here!" he sputters.

"Are you saying I should go?"

"Of course not! You're always welcome to stay." He leans in again, closing his eyes.

I shove him in the chest. "What't the matter with you?" He stubbornly doesn't move, keeping himself firmly between me and the typewriter.

The hairs on the back of my neck bristle. He's doing this on purpose! He knows the typewriter is a Touchstone!

"Who are you?" I demand. "And don't say Scout! Are you like Vera?" Now that I know the Watcher's name, I can use it.

"I don't know what you mean." Scout's voice is level. He looks serious. And like he's lying.

"You're bad at lying, you know. They should have picked someone else for this job. And this is your real job, right, following me, checking up on me?"

"Why would I follow you around? A bit full of yourself, aren't you? You're beginning to sound like a loon."

"Are you saying you're not a Watcher?" There I've said it. And I grab his arm as I do, pushing him toward the typewriter. He can disappear first!

"Stop it!" Scout pulls back, twisting out of my grip.

"I know the truth about Vera. My mother told me. So you might as well tell me the truth, too!"

"Serena told you?" He searches my eyes. "What did she say?"

I take a deep breath and tell him everything. Either he's a Watcher or he'll think I'm a nut job. But I'm betting he's a Watcher. Suddenly, I'm certain of it.

Sure enough, Scout nods and sighs. "Okay, you know everything now. And you're right, I'm a Watcher, but I was sent to protect you, to make sure nothing happened to you. Your mother can't be in the same place as you, so someone else had to take this job."

"So there's a reason you remind me of Claude from Paris, Giovanni from Rome, Clark from London." My voice trembles.

Scout shrugs. "One and the same, yes."

"But how?" I press.

"I use contacts to change eye color, dye to change my hair, small tricks like that. Just changing posture, voices, gestures can make you seem like another person. I'm good at what I do."

"But you were so mad at me in Paris for disappearing when

all along you knew I was a time-traveler! And how did you look so much older?" I feel like my head is going to explode. First Mom telling me the truth about Vera and now this!

"Makeup works in a pinch. I only needed to use it that once, for a very short time. Look, Mira, I never meant to hurt you. My job has always been to protect you. And I hope that one day, when this is all over, we can be friends. Real ones."

It's jarring to hear him use my name. It doesn't belong in this time. "If you were supposed to protect me, how come I ended up in prison – twice?"

"I tried! And I helped get you out. You're here now and totally fine, so clearly I did my job. So far." Scout holds my gaze, his eyes warm and familiar. He's the same boy I kissed in Paris, the same one I reached for in Rome. Can we really be friends, like he says?

"Who are you really? What time do you belong in?"

Scout takes both by hands in his. "Yours. My real name is Ari and I was born a few years before you, here, in San Francisco. This really is my city. We might actually meet in our present like normal people."

"Except we aren't normal people."

"No," he says. "We aren't." And this time, when he leans in for a kiss, I tilt my face up to meet his lips.

Time stops and all I feel is the warmth of his mouth on mine. When we finally pull apart, I shiver. "I have to go," I whisper.

Scout – or Ari – looks down at the ground, then up at me. "If you need me, I'll be there for you. I promise."

I nod and reach out to the typewriter, thrusting through the shimmering waves of color and light to touch the cold metal. A sharp jolt rolls and rumbles, like an earthquake all around me, space and light heaving and shifting with a low sound like the ocean pounding in my ears.

April 18, 1906

At first I think I'm still whirling through the years. The air is thick with smoke and dull thuds rock the ground, but this has to be the 1906 earthquake. Piles of brick and rubble are all that's left of some buildings. Some still stand, but lean crazily, as if a giant has shoved them to one side. Carts lie tipped over in the street, and people surge around me, like hollow-eyed zombies, their possessions loaded in baskets, sheets, carts, whatever they could find to drag with them. I look toward the bay, but a grey haze of dust and smoke blocks the view. The air tastes like brick and ash and smells heavy and bitter all at once, like lime from all the crushed concrete. It feels like the end of the world, like some horrible nightmare.

Is the whole city destroyed? I try to remember the map that Malcolm showed me, ages ago when we first got back to Berkeley. A hotel across the street still has one wall and the bank next to it looks okay, so the fires haven't spread yet. Panic shoots through me. As bad as it is, it's going to get worse.

I've been in earthquakes before and it's always unnerving to

feel the ground roll under your feet. What should be solid, suddenly isn't. But this is different. This is complete destruction. I jump over a deep crack, pulling the street apart.

How will I ever find Mom and what can the Watcher want here? There's nothing to censor, just panic and destruction.

It's hard to recognize streets like this, strewn with bricks and glass. The old structure that used to house the newspaper is gone, a pile. I stare at it, hoping nobody was inside.

I keep walking, numbly, not sure where to go. A proclamation posted on one of the few lamp posts still standing warns that looters will be shot on sight. I shiver as I remember what Dad said – that people carrying their own belongings were killed.

Why come here? This is much worse than London when it was bombed in World War I. The whole downtown has collapsed.

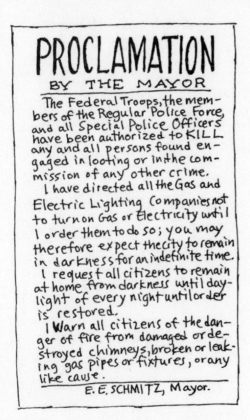

A horse lies dead in the street, a wagon turned on its side behind it. I shudder and swallow a sob. It feels like San Francisco itself is dying. The city I love so much is shattered.

Some men with a fruit cart walk toward me. I watch them, dazed. They seem purposeful, intent, not like the grieving refugees, stumbling toward safety. The cart, the horses, remind me of something – suddenly I remember the Watcher tipping over a similar cart in 1864, something about stopping a man from setting up a bank.

And sure enough, there she is behind the cart, the Watcher. Vera.

She's dressed as elegantly as ever, though her light blue dress is frosted pink with brick dust, and her hair is loose, not its usual stylish, carefully arranged bun. She looks even more determined than the men do, guiding the horses through the rubble.

Seeing her, I'm filled with purpose amidst all the destruction. I can't save San Francisco now, but I can save its future. I run up to her, dodging piles of wreckage.

"You, there!" I call, determined to finally get things right.

The Watcher sees me, but she doesn't answer. Instead, she rushes toward the cart. Is she trying to tip it again? What is it with her and fruit carts? One man pushes her back. Another shields the cart. All this for some oranges?

I want to grab her, throw her to the ground, but she's strong, stronger than I am. There has to be another way to stop her. And then, I know what to do.

I run up to her and take her hand, all sugary concern, hustling her away from the cart. She's so shocked by my embrace, she doesn't fight me. "Aunt Vera, don't worry, I'll get you to a safe place." I smile at the men protecting their oranges. "Please forgive my aunt. The earthquake has quite unhinged her. She didn't mean any harm."

"Watch out for her," one man snarls. "Haven't you seen the signs? Thieving won't be tolerated!"

The Watcher says nothing, her mouth a tight line. Her eyes are full of smoldering rage and I expect she'll claw at me as soon as the men are gone. She stares at me for a long minute as the cart rumbles away.

"What do you think you're doing?! You've interfered for the last time!" She whips her hand away and runs toward a clock, teetering in the street, like a misplaced toy in a dollhouse. "This time, I'll get her! Your mother is mine!"

I grab for her, but she's fast. Before I can get her, she reaches out, touches the clock, and vanishes in a shimmer of blue and gold.

That's just what Mom said – our chances are running out. Whatever happens next won't be now, it'll be whenever the Watcher goes to. I take one last look at the horror all around me. I hope the next time I see San Francisco, the city will have recovered all its charms.

I reach out and touch the same clock as the Watcher, and time collapses around me, dust whirls, a deafening roar fills my ears, and then suddenly everything is silent.

April 18, 1934

This San Francisco is much closer to the one I know. All signs of the quake are gone. Buildings gleam in the spring sunlight, the sidewalk glitters, and the air is fresh and clean, not choked with dust and smoke. There are cars now – big bulbous ones – and traffic lights. I'm still wearing a dress, but it's shorter and my shoes are

more comfortable, if uglier. They have a clunky boxiness to them, like everything in this time. Lotta's Fountain is here, but I could swear it was across the street before, on Geary, when I first touched it with Malcolm. Could this be an alternative reality, the world after it's been ruined by the Watcher?

My stomach pitches. Does that mean the Watcher got Mom? I try to calm down, to think clearly, but I can taste panic, a sharp metallic tang.

Men in hats with briefcases stride by. Women wearing short white gloves and bouncy hair amble slowly. I just stand there, trying to figure out what to do next.

I start walking down Market, toward the Ferry Building. I want to be close to the water, to see the bay. The water lies flat in front of me, still no bridges, but Alcatraz sports the white walls of the prison now.

"Mira!"

I whip my head around. Someone's calling my name? Someone knows me here?

"Mira!"

And then I see her. It's Mom! She's okay, the Watcher didn't get her! I run to her, throwing myself at her as if I were a toddler, not a 14-year-old.

"You did just the right thing!" Mom says. "You kept Vera from the gold."

"Gold? There was no gold." I want to savor Mom's praise, because I did keep Vera away from the cart, but she must have picked the wrong cart because all I saw was fruit.

"Under the oranges. One of those men was Amadeo Giannini, the fruit-seller's son. He had a small bank, the Bank of Italy, and he was the only one to get his deposits out of downtown before the fires made the vaults so hot, it would take weeks before they cooled down enough to open."

"So he hid all his gold under the oranges?"

"Exactly! And because he had access to money when nobody else did, he ran his bank from a plank across two barrels in the middle of the street, offering loans to people and businesses quickly so they could rebuild after the earthquake."

"So the Watcher didn't want San Francisco rebuilt? What does that have to do with censorship?" The more Mom tells me, the less I understand.

"No, that's not what she was trying to stop. She didn't want Giannini to be so successful. His was the only bank open for weeks after the earthquake. Everyone who took out a loan from him paid it back. His bank grew and now it's one of the biggest in the world. Bank of America."

"I can understand hating banks, but still, why care about that one in particular?"

"Because that bank will finance one of the most important projects in San Francisco, in California. The Golden Gate Bridge, a symbol of freedom and opportunity for everyone. And a place where some important events need to happen, far in the future."

"So without the gold in the orange cart, no Bank of America, and without the Bank of America, no Golden Gate Bridge?" I look across the bay. "But there's still no bridge, so we didn't stop the Watcher. Wow, that's something, censoring a bridge!"

"Not yet, but we will." Mom takes my hand and pulls me to the front of the Ferry Building. She hails a cab as if we belong in this time.

We drive along the edge of the bay. It feels like we're in the middle of an old black-and-white movie, except everything's in color. This is the closest we've come to my own present and it feels really odd, much more risky somehow. There's no Exploratorium, no Pier 39, just warehouses, piers, a gritty business kind of place, not a pretty touristy place. Except for the beautiful water, the hills of Marin in the distance, the gleaming walls of Alcatraz.

The cab stops at the edge of the city, by a big park. There's nothing around us, nothing.

"Come on," Mom says. "From here we have to walk." She pays the cab driver and I wonder where she got the money. More time-travel skills she never told me about?

"Okay, explain all this to me. Where are we going? And why?"

"You'll see."

"Mom, enough already! Just tell me!"

Mom points to the construction site below us. There are strange-looking rollers, cranes, big wheels of cables, and steel rods stacked up like lumber, all near some massive block of concrete on the edge of the cliff. It's the beginning of the Golden Gate Bridge!

"So she didn't stop it! It's being built!" Books are easier to burn than bridges (despite that expression).

Did we need to bother to follow the Watcher here? What could she possibly do?

"She's still trying. Come on!" Mom yanks my arm and hurries us closer to the huge concrete base that will anchor the bridge to the San Francisco side.

There's a lot of machinery, but no people.

"Where did everyone go?" I ask. "Did Vera get rid of the workers?"

"They've gone home for the day," Mom says. "Look!"

And there she is, Vera, below us by the side of the concrete pier. She's carrying a briefcase.

"I'll grab the bomb, you grab Vera," Mom whispers, gesturing for me to go around the other side so that we surround her.

"Bomb?!"

"We have to do this, Mira, now!"

Vera's a terrorist herself now? I feel dizzy and sick. Malcolm was right – Mom's trying to stop a terrorist attack, this one, right now.

Somehow thinking of my brother gives me strength. I have to do this for him, for Dad. And for Mom. I sneak around behind the Watcher as she sets the briefcase down at the base of the pier. She'd need a lot of explosives to blow up that much concrete.

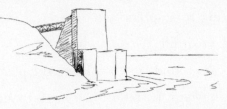

My mouth feels dry, full of ashes.

Mom runs down the slope in front of Vera. "You can have me now, just don't set off the bomb. Take me instead!"

"You?" the Watcher sneers. "I'll deal with you AFTER I destroy the bridge. Part of the pleasure will be having you watch."

"You don't have to do this, Vera. You're crossing a line now. Before you shut down words, books, stories. But a bridge?"

"You know as well as I do what this bridge stands for – and what will happen on it in the future if I don't get rid of it now. I'm helping people, protecting them."

I've been creeping up, hidden by the construction crates and piles of pipe until I'm close enough to see the specks of saliva flying from the Watcher's mouth. The two women face each other, hands clenched, eyes flashing. They're like mirror images of each other, each absolutely sure she's right and the other one is wrong.

"You can't stop me!" Vera sneers.

"Maybe not me alone," Mom says.

The Watcher whips her head back and all my doubt and confusion evaporate. I run out from behind the pipes, flinging us both to the ground.

Mom snatches the briefcase and throws it as far as she can into the bay.

"Noooo!" Vera howls. She reaches for something in her pocket. I wrestle with her, trying to stop her, but she's fast. She frantically pushes a button and a roar fills the air.

I'm thrown back onto the ground, almost hitting the pier, as a huge swell of water blasts upward, then out, turning into an explosive wave. The water crashes onto the ground around me, pulling me back with it, swallowing me in its freezing blackness. I claw the ground, reaching for something to hold onto, struggling against the wave.

And then the water's gone, sucked back into the bay.

I sit up, coughing out sea water in wracking gulps.

Where's Mom? And the Watcher? Were they dragged out to sea?

Then I see a body at the base of the pier and I stumble toward it, crying.

"Mom! Mom, are you okay?"

I lean over the woman with dark curly hair. And feel nauseous. It's not Mom. It's the Watcher.

She pulls herself up, gagging and retching.

"I still have time, lots of time. All the time in the world!" she hisses. "The bridge doesn't matter. It can have its shining moment in history. There's always something else I can do."

A sea lion lurches out of the bay. No, it's a person. It's Mom! She lunges at Vera. "Your time is up!"

The Watcher stands up, facing Mom with steely determination. "I'm saving people, protecting them! Don't you understand how hurtful language can be? How much damage a drawing can do?"

"You're wrong, Vera. You're not saving people. You're suffocating them!"

"What would you know about caring for people? You left your own children to chase me! You have a cold heart, Serena."

"No, she doesn't!" I roar, running at her.

"You're pathetic!" The Watcher sneers. "You can't stop me, neither of you."

Mom grabs Vera's arm. "Together we can. Now, Mira, now! Pull her to the pier!"

For a second, a minute, a year, I'm frozen. The bay lies flat in front of me, the sky arches bright blue overhead. Then I reach out, not for a Touchstone this time, but for the Watcher. I grip her other arm, yanking it to the concrete just as Mom does the same.

An ear-splitting scream tears the air. My stomach pitches in panic – is that Mom? But it's the Watcher, her face contorted in agony.

For a minute, I think she'll melt away like the Wicked Witch of the West. Instead, strange lights wrap around her, tighter and tighter, flashing bolts of green and gold, purple and orange. Her stylish clothes melt away and instead she wears a dark, tattered dress and wooden shoes. Through it all, I don't let go until suddenly there's a clap of thunder, a flash of lightning right through me and I'm thrown back onto the ground again.

When I come to, it's still 1934. I'm still at Fort Point, still by the base of the beginnings of the Golden Gate Bridge. My head feels light and I sit up unsteadily. My clothes are wet and cold and I shiver in the deepening shadows.

Mom is sitting next to me, looking at the bay and smiling. The Watcher has vanished.

"What happened?" I whisper.

"We did it. I thought we could, but I wasn't sure. Vera was strong, but the two of us together, we were stronger. When we both made her touch the cement pier, that stripped her of her time-travel ability, throwing her back to her original time and place, where she'll stay."

"Where's that?" I ask, my voice hoarse.

"A village outside of London in the early 1300s."

"She was from the Middle Ages?" She seemed so capable, so modern. I can't help admiring her, just a little. She'd escaped her original culture so well. "So time-travelers can lose their talent?" I did that? I took away her power?

"Yes, but you see how hard it is! And all that time-travel energy has to go somewhere. That's why we had to make her touch the bridge, well, it will be the bridge."

"I don't get it. Why?" I'm shaking with the enormity of what just happened. I've condemned Vera to life in medieval England where she'll probably die of the plague. But I've stopped her from any more censorship.

"Now the pier holds that energy." Mom smiles at me, a sunny smile that warms me up, steadies the shivering. "The Golden Gate Bridge is a Touchstone. Thanks to you and me – and Vera."

"So that's how Touchstones are made. Malcolm wanted to know." A bubble of happiness floats up through me. I did it! We've done it!

"There's a balance in the world. Whenever a time-traveler dies or, more rarely, loses their gift, a Touchstone is born. And whenever a Touchstone is destroyed, a new time-traveler is born."

I hate to think that something had to be lost for me to be able to time-travel. But I'm feeling pretty lucky right now – and, finally, like a true time-traveler.

"So now can we go home?" I ask. I'm eager to see Malcolm, to let him know everything that's happened. And Dad, too, of course.

"I hope so. I don't know how weak we are after taking away Vera's power and giving it to the bridge. But we can try, and this time, we should do it together." Mom gets up, dusts the sand off her skirt and leans over to pull me up. My hand still tingles, but the dizziness is gone.

And there, before us, the buttress glows a cool blue and silver. The familiar magnetic draw of a Touchstone.

"Ready?" Mom asks.

I nod.

And together again, we touch the pier.

July 15

We're back on Market Street in the old, familiar San Francisco – or I should say, new, modern San Francisco. The Muni bus rumbles by and a musician wearing a tie-dye shirt serenades the tourists. He's singing *California Dreaming*, the kind of hoky song that fits in with the city's clichéd image (and his '60s retro clothes). Normally, I'd make some kind of wisecrack, but today, the song

feels perfect. There's no place else I'd rather be. I'm back in my dry jeans and T-shirt, my comfortable shoes. And the sun is high in the sky, beaming down its warmth.

Mom looks dazed. "Where's the nearest BART

station? I'm a little turned around."

"First let's get Malcolm. He should be in that cafe across the street."

"Malcolm's here!" Mom smiles through her exhaustion.

"Yeah, he always helps me out like this when I time-travel. We're a team."

"I'm so glad." Mom takes my arm, a very un-Mom-like thing to do, and we cross the street together.

Malcolm is just where I left him, still at his laptop, still wearing earbuds. But this time I don't have to yank them out of his ears. He looks up at the doorway just as we walk in.

"Mom!" he yelps. He flings off the earbuds and runs to give her a tight hug. Then it's my turn. "You did it!" he whispers into my ear.

"*We* did it!" I whisper back.

"Come on, tell me everything! Everything!" Malcolm is so excited, he can't stop moving. He hugs Mom again and for a minute I think he's going to cry. Instead he lets go, grabs a chair for Mom, pulls one out for me, and clears away the laptop, a blur of motion.

"Shouldn't we talk to your father first?" Mom asks.

"Oh, yeah! Dad's been so worried. I'll text him, so he knows you're both here. But I can't wait until we see him – you've got to tell me everything's okay!"

"It is, Malcolm," I assure him. "Nothing was quite what we expected. But you were right about a lot of things!"

"So explain!"

Mom does most of the talking. I just add in the details she doesn't know – like the times I talked to the Watcher, what she said. And about Scout being yet another Watcher, only more like a Guardian Angel. It's a lot for Malcolm to take in. Even for me, hearing Mom lay it out again.

By the time Mom's finished, Malcolm's heard back from Dad. "He's in Marin and he's on his way."

"Marin? That's perfect" Mom says. "Tell him we'll meet him on the Golden Gate Bridge."

"The bridge?" I ask, dazed. Oh yeah, it's finally been built.

"Seems right, doesn't it?" Mom asks.

And it does.

We take a cab to the southern entrance like we did a century ago. The pier that Mom and I touched is below us, supporting this end of the span. We walk out onto the path that didn't exist the last time we were here. I've always loved crossing this bridge. It's one of the most beautiful places I know. And now it feels more beautiful than ever. Malcolm peppers us with questions while we head north.

What was Mark Twain's talk like? What did we see during the earthquake? How much damage was there really?

Some things I can answer. Others I don't know. One thing I do know, though, is that this bridge definitely had to be built. Not just because connecting people and towns matter, but because art does. From funny stories about jumping frogs to magnificent structures.

Dad runs to us from where he's parked the car on the Marin side. We meet in the middle, and stand there, leaning on the railing, looking back at the shimmering city, the buildings gleaming silver and white like the magical Emerald City of Oz.

Mom and Dad hug tightly without saying a word. Malcolm's smile is so wide, he looks goofy. And me, I feel deeply at peace. This is the perfect time and place for me. Right here, right now. And there's not one thing I'd change.

Author's Note:

The basic outlines of Mark Twain's early writing career as described by Mira are factual. Samuel Clemens first worked as a journalist for the Virginia City *Territorial Enterprise* in 1862 and it was in that newspaper that his famous pen name first appeared. He left Washoe (as Nevada Territory was then called) for San Francisco with his good friend, Steve Gillis, after a failed duel with a rival newspaperman. Although both sides agreed not to fight at the last minute, a judge still threatened to make Clemens an example under a new anti-dueling law. Rather than face the risk of punishment, Clemens left for the big city.

The University of California at Berkeley houses the Mark Twain Project, a treasure trove of letters, manuscripts, and newspaper articles. For more concrete artifacts, you can still see the old printing press, desks, and files at the old offices of the *Territorial Enterprise* in Virginia City, Nevada, now called the Mark Twain Museum.

Although much of Mark Twain's conversation is invented, the biographical facts and newspaper stories are all real, from the one about the earthquake to the one about an early visit to the Cliff House to the unpublished one about the bullies attacking a Chinese-American laundryman. The arc of his career is also real, including his stint as a reporter in Hawaii (then called the Sandwich Islands) and the lectures he did after his return. The language on the poster Mira sketches is the actual text, calling for the doors to open at seven, with the trouble to start at eight.

Mark Twain's actual language appears on p.31-32 (the earth-quake article), p.50 (the description of police detectives), p.71-72 (the fall of fruit story), p.95-96 (the description of Jews in Hannibal), p.115 (the story about the attack on the Chinese laundryman), and p.153 (the description of sea-sickness).

San Francisco offered new starts to many people. Groups that faced prejudice in other parts of the country could thrive there and odd personalities were not only tolerated, they were often supported. One such character was Emperor Norton, the bicyclist wearing the grungy uniform that Mira sketches when she first arrives in 1864 San Francisco. Born in England, Joshua Abraham Norton came to the city in 1849 already a millionaire from a family inheritance. Unfortunately, he lost his fortune in risky speculations. He kept his pride and dignity, however, proclaiming himself Norton I, Emperor of the United States. He slept in cheap rooming houses, ate at free lunch counters (like those Mira describes), coined his own money which merchants accepted at face value, and directed government through his many declarations. His proclamations were grandiose, especially the ones calling for a bridge to be built across the bay.

The two dogs, Bummer and Lazarus, that followed him everywhere were also accepted as city mascots and when they died, the mutts were given magnificent funerals. Mark Twain described Lazarus' funeral, as did other reporters, and cartoonists featured them in drawings for newspapers. Norton himself provided the model for the character of King in Mark Twain's *Adventures of Huckleberry Finn*. Robert Louis Stevenson also based a character on the emperor in his book, *The Wrecker*.

Norton was taken so seriously that the 1870 U.S. Census described his occupation as "Emperor."

When he died, the Pacific Club collected enough money for a fine coffin and extravagant funeral. The cortege of mourners following the hearse stretched over two miles and more than 10,000 people lined the streets to give the Emperor the send-off he deserved.

Ina Coolbrith really does have a park named after her in San Francisco, not far from the house where she lived on Taylor Street. Born in Illinois, Ina was the niece of Joseph Smith, the founder of the Mormon Church. After her father was killed by an anti-polygamy mob (he had married twenty to thirty women by then), Ina's mother left the church and started a new life in Southern California. Ina wrote her first poems as an eleven-year-old in their new home, and had one published in the newspaper when she was only fifteen.

Ina grew into a renowned beauty and at seventeen was married to an ironworker who proved abusive. After the death of their baby, Ina left her husband in a sensational divorce trial, one of her many brave public stances. Once again, she moved, this time to San Francisco, where she quickly met a group of writers including Bret Harte and Sam Clemens. Her poems were widely acclaimed and through them she met Alfred Lord Tennyson, John Muir, and Charles Stoddard, to name only a few. She, Harte, and Stoddard worked together as editors of the *Overland Monthly*. The three of them were known as the "Golden Gate Trinity," the arbiters of literary taste in San Francisco. Coolbrith was so highly respected, she was elected an honorary member of the Bohemian Club, which to this date doesn't allow women in their society (though there have been four honorary members early in the club's history).

Although Ina continued to publish books of her poetry and hold literary evenings, in order to support her family, she moved to Oakland to work in the public library. But San Francisco was her true cultural home and when the position of librarian at the San Francisco Public Library opened up, her friends urged her to apply. Unfortunately, since the job was reserved for men, she couldn't. Instead, the San Francisco Mercantile Library Association offered her the position — which meant Ina was living in the city during the 1906 earthquake. Her home and her enormous collection of books, including the one she was writing on her own life and the California literary scene, were all destroyed.

In preparation for the 1915 Panama-Pacific International Exposition, it was decided to name her State Poet Laureate and she was crowned by the then-president of the University of California, Benjamin Ide Wheeler. When the Exposition moved to San Diego, an authors' day was added, celebrating thirteen California writers. November 2nd was named Ina Coolbrith Day in her honor.

Jews found a home remarkably free of prejudice in early San Francisco and many of the important founders of the city came from Germany and Eastern Europe. The cemetery Mira describes near Mission Dolores was one of the earliest Jewish burial grounds in the city. Land quickly became too valuable to use for the dead, however, and in 1900 no more cemeteries were allowed within city limits. The pressure of population growth inspired another ordinance in 1912 which evicted all then-existing cemeteries. Most moved to Colma, a town south of San Francisco, which became known as having more dead bodies in it than living ones. Some were moved to Mountain View Cemetery across the bay in Oakland. The graves of Emperor Norton and Levi Strauss were both moved to Colma, nicknamed the City of the Silent.

The 1906 earthquake struck early on April 18. Fires raged for several days and 80% of the city was destroyed. Three thousand people died and around three hundred thousand were left homeless. The history of the misuse of dynamite following the 1906 earthquake is well-documented, and the transformation of Amadeo Giannini's small Bank of Italy into the giant Bank of America indeed grew out of early loans made after the disaster, thanks to Giannini's quick thinking in getting the bank's assets safely out of the vault before the fires started. The Bank of America went on to finance the bonds that allowed for the construction of the Golden Gate Bridge, one of the most recognized landmarks in the world.

Bibliography:

Allen, Annalee. *Oakland,* Arcadia Publishing, South Carolina, 2005.

Barker, Malcolm. *San Francisco Memoirs, 1835-1851,* Londonborn Publications, San Francisco, 1994.

Benson, Ivan. *Mark Twain's Western Years,* Russell & Russell, New York, 1938.

Birt, Rodger C. *History's Anteroom: Photography in San Francisco 1906-1909,* William Stout Publishers, Richmond California 2011.

Bowman, John S. editor, *The American West Year by Year,* Crescent Books, New York, 1995.

Branch, Edgar Marquess. *The Literary Apprenticeship of Mark Twain,* Russell & Russell, New York 1966.

Brown, Allen. *Golden Gate,* Doubleday & Co., New York, 1965.

Browning, Peter. Yerba Buena, *San Francisco, From the Beginning to the Gold Rush, 1769-1849,* Great West Books, Lafayette, California, 1998.

Chartier, JoAnn and Enss, Chris. *With Great Hope: Women of the California Gold Rush,* Falcon Publishing, Helena, Montana, 2000.

Dicker, Laverne Mau. *The Chinese in San Francisco: A Pictorial History,* Dover Publications, New York, 1979.

Fracchia, Charles. *Fire & Gold: The San Francisco Story,* Heritage Media Corp, Encinitas, California 1996.

Hastings, Lansford. *The Emigrants' Guide to Oregon and California,* Applewood Books, Bedford, Massachusetts, 1994.

Isaac, Frederick. *Jews of Oakland and Berkeley,* Arcadia Publishing, San Francisco, 2009.

Johnson, Drew Heath and Eymann, Marcia. *Silver & Gold: Case Images of the California Gold Rush,* University of Iowa Press, 1998.

Library of Congress video of San Francisco earthquake from April 18, 1906: http://www.loc.gov/item/00694425

Lotchin, Roger. *San Francisco, 1846-1856, from Hamlet to City,* University of Illinois Press, Chicago, 1997.

Macdonald, Donald and Nadel, Ira. *Golden Gate Bridge: History of Design of an Icon,* Chronicle Books, San Francisco, 2008.

Marks, Paula Mitchell. *Precious Dust: The True Saga of the Western Gold Rushes,* Harper Collins West, New York, 1995.

Margolin, Reuben, editor. *Bret Harte's Gold Rush,* Heyday Books, Berkeley, 1997.

Martini, John Arturo. *Fortress Alcatraz, Guardian of the Golden Gate,* Ten Speed Press, Berkeley, 1990.

McCunn, Ruthanne Lum. *Chinese American Portraits,* Chronicle Books, San Francisco, 1988.

Miller Christine. *San Francisco's Financial District,* Arcadia Publishing, San Francisco, 2005.

Muscantine, Doris. *Old San Francisco: the Biography of a City from Early Days to the Earthquake,* G.P. Putnam's Sons, New York, 1975.

Neider, Charles, editor. *Life as I Find It: A Treasury of Mark Twain Rarities,* Cooper Square Press, New York, 1961.

Quirk, Tom, editor. *The Portable Mark Twain,* Penguin Books, New York, 1951.

Rasmussen, R. Kent, editor, *Mark Twain: Autobiographical Writings,* Penguin Books, New York, 2012.

Rickard, T. K. editor. *After Earthquake and Fire: A Reprint of the Articles and Editorial Comment Appearing in the Mining and Scientific Press Immediately After the Disaster at San Francisco, April 18, 1906,* Mining & Scientific Press, San Francisco, 1906.

Richards, Rand. *Historic San Francisco: A Concise History and Guide,* Heritage House Publishers, San Francisco, 1991.

Royce, Sarah. *A Frontier Lady: Recollections of the Gold Rush and Early California,* Yale University Press, 1932.

Schwartz, Richard. *Earthquake Exodus, 1906,* RSB Books, Berkeley, California, 2005.

Smith, Dennis. *San Francisco is Burning,* Viking, New York, 2005.

Smith, Harriet Elinor, editor. *Autobiography of Mark Twain*, University of California Press, Berkeley, 2010, Vols. 1 & 2.

Starr, Kevin. *Golden Gate: The Life and Times of America's Greatest Bridge*, Bloomsbury Press, New York, 2010.

Street Frames, *Eyewitness Accounts of the 1906 San Francisco Earthquake and Fire, A Commemorative Book by the Daughters of Charity*, Los Altos Hills, California 2005.

Taper, Bernard, editor. *Mark Twain's San Francisco*, Heyday Books, Berkeley, 2003.

Tchen, John Kuo Wei. *Genthe's Photographs of San Francisco's Old Chinatown*, Dover Publications, Toronto, 1984.

Thomas, Gordon and Witts, Max Morgan. *The San Francisco Earthquake*, Stein and Day, New York, 1971.

Twain, Mark. *A Connecticut Yankee in King Arthur's Court*, Oxford University Press, Oxford, 1997.

Twain, Mark. *How Nancy Jackson Married Kate Wilson and Other Tales of Rebellious Girls and Daring Young Women*, University of Nebraska Press, Lincoln, 2001.

Twain, Mark. *The Innocents Abroad*, The Modern Library, New York, 2003.

Twain, Mark. *Mark Twain's San Francisco, Being a Generous and Uninhibited Cornucopia of Reports, Speculations, Satires, Brickbats, Musings, Topical Verse, and Other Observations*, Heydey Books, Berkeley, California 2003.

Twain, Mark, edited by Anderson, Frederic. *A Pen Warmed-Up in Hell,*

Harper Colophon Books, New York, 1972.

Twain, Mark. *Roughing It,* Signet Classics, New York, 2008.

Van der Zee, John. *Gate: The True Story of the Design and Construction of the Golden Gate Bridge,* Simon & Schuster, New York, 1986.

Vincent, Stephen, editor. *Uncertain Country: The Wingate Letters,* University of California, Berkeley, 2000.

Ward, Geoffrey C. and Duncan, Dayton. *Mark Twain,* Knopf, New York, 2001.

Watkins, T.H. and Olmsted, R. R. *Mirror of the Dream: An Illustrated History of San Francisco,* Scrimshaw Press, San Francisco, 1976.

Willes, Burl, editor. *Picturing Berkeley: a Postcard History,* Gibbs Smith Publisher, Salt Lake City, 2005.

Williams, George J. *On the Road with Mark Twain in California and Nevada,* Tree By The River Publishing, Dayton, Nevada, 1993.

Acknowledgements

Every writer needs a writing group. I'm very fortunate to have such talented readers in mine. This book wouldn't be as strong without the careful comments of Gennifer Choldenko, Diane Fraser, and Emily Polsby. Elias Stahl, Kristen Carvalho, and Joan Lester also provided helpful criticism. But I owe the most to Asa Stahl, whose sharp editorial eye shaped this book through its many revisions.

About the Author

Marissa Moss has written more than 50 books for children. Her popular *Amelia's Notebook* series has sold millions of copies and been translated into five languages. The author has won many awards, including ALA Notable, Best Books in Booklist, Amelia Bloomer Pick of the List, and the California Book Award. Mira's previous adventure, *Mira's Diary: Home Sweet Rome*, was a finalist for the Northern California Book Reviewers' Award.

Read Mira's Other Adventures

Published by Sourcebooks:

Mira's Diary:
Lost in Paris (1)

Mira's Diary:
Home Sweet Rome (2)

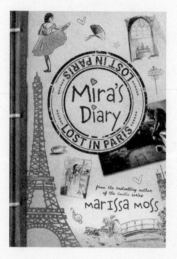

Published by Creston Books:
Mira's Diary:
Bombs Over London (3)

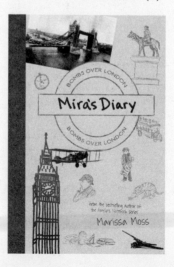

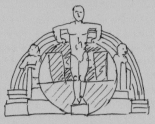

Pacific Stock Exchange,
1929-30, 155 Sansome

How far into the past can you go?

Alaska Commercial Building,
1908, 350 California Street

Standard Oil Co. Building,
1922, 225 Bush Street

1930, 130 Montgomery

Russ Building,
1927, 235 Montgomery

Robert Dollar Building,
1919, 311 California